TH... SIDE OF HELL

Patrick C. Harrison III

This is a work of fiction. None of the people, places, or events described in this novel actually exist or happened. Not yet anyway...

PC3 HORROR

pc3horror.com
Instagram@thepc3
Etsy.com/shop/pc3books
Slasher@PC3
pc3horror.substack.com
pc3@pc3horror.com

DEDICATION

For Aron Beauregard

CONTENTS

ACKNOWLEDGMENTS

Thank you to everyone keeping indie horror—splatterpunk and extreme horror, in particular—alive. Thank you to all the authors, publishers, editors, and artists for the content. But most of all, thank you to the readers. Despite what some may say, books will never die. And it's you, readers, we can all thank for that.

ONE

The first time they went, nobody got hurt, nobody died, and nobody had any body parts lopped off or destroyed beyond repair. Nobody was really even scared until the end. The first time they went, that is.

The headlights swung around with the curve of the dirt road, temporarily illuminating clusters of yellowing autumn leaves. Then the trees were dark again and getting distant in the rearview, a kicked-up cloud of dust floating through them like a billowing fog. The man's hands were tight on the steering wheel and his foot mashed down on the pedal. The Mercedes roared as best it could.

"Slow down, Jim," Mona said, crossing her arms across her chest and shaking her head. "You're gonna get us killed."

"Oh, shut-up," Jim muttered between gritted teeth, his hands gripping tighter on the wheel. *I should have taken one fuckin' bump before leaving the house*, he thought, *just to take the edge off*.

"Dickhead," Mona said under her breath.

Jim cut his eyes at her, wanting her to see his scowl, but she was watching the moonlit woods blur by outside her window.

"Are we lost?" Mamie groaned from the backseat.

Jim glared at her in the rearview, then looked over at the boy, who was thankfully occupied with his cellphone. "We're not lost. I saw a sign right back there." He took a deep breath, trying to relax, reminding himself this was *his* bloody idea; none of the others exactly jumped with excitement to go out tonight.

"We seem lost."

"We're not lost, goddammit!" he growled.

"Ooookay. No need to lose your shit, Dad." Mamie rolled her eyes.

"Watch your mouth, young lady!" Mona said, whipping her head around to her daughter and pointing a sharp finger at her.

"I'm six-FUCKING-teen, Mom! I can say what I want!"

"Not as long as you live under my roof. And, besides, Julian doesn't need to be exposed to that kind of talk."

"Are you serious?" Mamie laughed, cutting her eyes over at her thirteen-year-old brother. "You and Dad cuss around him all the time. Anyway, he's so absorbed in his stupid game he wouldn't know it if I lit his fucking hair on fire."

"Not true," Julian said, not lifting his gaze from his phone. "That would make it very hard to concentrate on the game."

Mamie snorted laughter.

Mona did the same, covering her mouth and trying not to show the spreading smile. "Just try not to say such things around your brother, okay?" she said between giggles.

Mamie sighed and nodded.

"See, we're here," Jim said triumphantly, seeing the sign come into view. "The Dark Side of Hell!"

The sign, hand-painted on a piece of warped particle board and nailed to a large oak, was dimly illuminated by a single green spotlight. Nailed to the same tree as the sign was a mangled bloody forearm, severed at the elbow, a piece of bone jutting out the end, a single finger pointing down the dark, dusty driveway beyond.

"Well, that's creepy," Mona said.

"That's awesome!" Mamie said.

"Yeah," agreed Jim. "With props like that, this haunted house might not be half bad."

"You sure that's a *prop*?" Mona said.

"It's a prop, dear."

"I don't know. I'm getting kinda scared, now."

"Don't be a wuss."

"Yeah, Mom," Mamie said, "don't be a pussy."

"Mamie," Mona yelled, "don't talk like that! Jim, where does she get that shit?"

"I can't imagine," Jim said passively, pulling the car into the driveway, taking another deep breath. He wasn't sure, but he thought there might be a couple of hydrocodones in the glove compartment. But what reason did he have to go digging through *there* with his family sitting all around him?

Gravel had long ago sunk into the ground of the driveway, and holes, desperately in need of fill, made even a slow approach feel like the jerky ascent of an old rollercoaster. Jim eyed his wife's bouncing breasts. She squawked an obscenity as her dyed-blonde hair fell in front of her face. Mamie, too, squawked an obscenity, but when Jim peaked at her in the rearview, she was laughing.

Julian said nothing, only moving his head as needed with the bounces, keeping his eyes always on his phone.

"Jesus Christ," Mona said, "how do they get any customers with a driveway like this?"

"Doesn't look like they get many," Jim said, pulling the Mercedes around a bend in the drive and past a collection of giant oaks. Beyond it was the haunted house (Jim's first impression was that it didn't deserve a name like The Dark Side of Hell; it was just an old fucking house with a handful of colored lights and cheap Halloween decorations thrown here and there) and a dirt parking lot with only one other car. Jim parked and sighed.

Mamie sighed too, then said, "Oh my god, this place is going to suck giant donkey dick."

"Mamie!" Mona yelled, brushing her hair from her face and pulling it into a bun. "Would you rather stay in the car?"

"Actually—"

"No, you're not staying in the car," Jim said. "Everyone get your asses out or I'm driving back home and y'all can spend your evening twiddling your goddamn thumbs."

No one moved. Jim held his hands up in a *Did you hear what I fuckin' said?* manner. Mona was eyeing her makeup in the mirror on the underside of her sun visor. Mamie chewed loudly on gum and crossed her arms over her tattered Wolftooth t-shirt and numerous dangling necklaces. Julian kept playing his game, as if the world around him no longer existed.

"Hello?" Jim said at last, looking from Mona—now painting on fresh lipstick—to Mamie—blowing a bubble between her black-painted lips and rolling her eyes.

"You suggested we could go home, Dad," Mamie

said.

"Everyone out! Let's have some fucking fun!"

Everyone opened their doors almost in unison. Only Julian lagged, because, Jim assumed, he was pausing or ending whatever game he was playing. Jim thought he might have to tell the kid to put the phone away but Julian did it on his own, sliding the device into his back pocket and looking at his surroundings for the first time, his eyebrows raised.

"Are you sure this is a spook house, Dad?" Julian said. "It just looks like a random trashy house with Halloween decorations."

"It's a haunted house, Julian," Jim said, trying to suppress his anger. "Didn't you see the cool sign with the arm back there?"

Julian shook his head. "The school's haunted house is better than this dump."

"Let's just give it a try. It's the week before Halloween for Christ's sake."

TWO

The house, in Mona's estimation, could have been built a hundred years ago or more. It was a sad wooden structure, not unlike the house she grew up in all those years ago in Mark's Point, not exactly the wealthy side of Mangle County. The haunted house was old and sad like her old house, yes, but there was something different about it. It wasn't simply the orange hues of light seeping from the windows, or the cheap Halloween decorations hung from trees and stapled to the rickety wooden fence of the backyard beyond. Something about the architecture suggested a unique style for this area of Texas. It was sharp, angular. Mamie would perhaps say it was gothic. Yes, Mona internally agreed, the house, despite not being particularly large, was gothic.

They'd only walked a dozen yards or so toward the front of the place, where an elderly gentleman in a top hat appeared to be napping in a fold-out chair when Jim snapped his fingers and turned back toward the car.

"Where are you going?" Mona said, continuing a slow stride toward the house.

"Might need some cash to get into the haunted house," he said, looking over his shoulder as he slowly jogged. "Got some in the glove box."

"I brought forty bucks," Mona said, slapping the back pocket of her jeans. "You told me to bring money, Jim."

"I'll pay," Jim said too cheerily, at the Mercedes now and opening the passenger door.

Mona rolled her eyes and turned back toward the house, the kids ahead of her now. She knew damn well why Jim was going back to the car. No doubt there were pills of some sort. Benzos or opioids or God only knew what. Maybe even a snort of cocaine or some mushrooms. *Lord, don't let it be acid*, she thought. *We'll never fucking get out of here if he's tripping on acid halfway through the spook house.*

She tucked her fingers into the shallow pockets of her jeans and continued slowly toward the house. Mamie and Julian had reached the wooden steps, flaked with white paint and warped, and they each stood at the base waiting, pulling their cellphones out and most certainly checking one social media site or another.

It was then, while sighing, Mona looked beyond the house, to the left of it, the west, the opposite side of which the backyard fence stretched for a ways. On this side of the house was a sliver of orange from the setting sun, barely enough to illuminate anything. But between that sliver of sun, the orange glow from the haunted house, and the flickering fire of a kerosene lantern on the porch, Mona could see the pumpkin patch planted there, a whole field worth. In this area of Texas it was commonplace to see fields of corn or cotton, even wheat. But pumpkins?

Not usually. But here they were, pumpkins of all shapes and sizes—fat and slender and small and large and round and smooshed-looking. All sorts. Unless her eyes were deceiving her, Mona thought she saw different shades of pumpkins too, mixed in amongst the orange, somewhat camouflaged beneath and between the spreading vines and green leaves of their plants. But, yes, there were maroon pumpkins and bluish pumpkins and off-white.

"How much are the pumpkins?" Mona asked, her eyes still on the field but her question directed to the old man on the porch, who she'd barely glanced at yet. Suddenly, for the first time in five or six years—since the kids were still young and innocent enough to be glowing globes of joy in her life—she wanted to carve a pumpkin. She wanted to make a beautiful, smiling jack-o'-lantern. Just like she'd done as a kid in Mark's Point.

"Ain't for sale," came the scratchy, smoker's voice of the old man.

Mona looked to him then, intending to ask why the hell not, but her words were caught in her throat when she finally laid good eye upon him. He was thin and, though he sat in an ages-old rocking chair, clearly tall. His suit was maybe dark blue or faded black, and it bore purple stripes that reminded Mona of the Joker. It was dirty and wrinkled, his necktie and top hat not much better, the whole getup matching his face perfectly. He was unshaven and weathered, the creases around his yellowish eyes seeming to drip into the rest of his sagging face.

"Ain't for sale," he said again, as if it needed repeating, displaying as he spoke his large, blocky teeth, stained a dark yellow, almost sickly orange, with grime from meals past stuck and hanging from them.

"You pay yet?" Jim said from behind, startling Mona in a way that seemed excessive, her heart suddenly thumping wildly.

"Jesus fuck, Jim," she said, sounding meaner than she meant.

"Nice language, Mom," Mamie said, both her and Julian looking up from their cellphones.

"Put your phones away," Mona snapped, then to Jim: "No, I didn't pay. You said you were getting cash."

"Right," Jim said, smiling and looking away, his lying look. "Well, turns out I didn't have any cash in the car. Thought I did. Sorry, babe."

Babe—a term Jim only used when he was full of shit. She rolled her eyes, reaching into her back pocket, producing two twenties. Her assumptions about why Jim went to the car were clearly correct. Turning back to the creepy old man, she asked what the entry fee was.

"Only five bucks apiece," the old man said, spreading his cracked lips into a smile that appeared, for a sudden horrifying second, carved into his face like a jack-o'-lantern, his dark yellow teeth looking like the guts of the pumpkin waiting to be pulled out before a little candle could be lit and placed within. "Just five bucks," he said again, just a creepy old man now.

Mona handed over a twenty without a word, the image of a flesh jack-o'-lantern still fresh on her mind.

"Thank you kindly, Miss . . ." he said, trailing off.

Mona didn't answer, taking a step backward, bumping into her husband.

"Gibson," Jim said, patting Mona on the shoulders and squeezing them. "We're the Gibsons."

"The motherfucking Gibsons," Julian said, his voice monotone, like the voice of a corpse.

"Julian!" Mona screeched, coming out of her trance like a bolt of lightning. She looked over just in time to see Jim's open palm smacking the back of the boy's head, his shaggy hair flying up and his head jolting forward. He held onto his phone though. Lord knew he wouldn't drop that fucking thing because of a little pop over the noggin.

THREE

Despite the pair of ten-milligram hydrocodones Jim chewed before entering The Dark Side of Hell, it still didn't amount to an enjoyable experience. They were barely halfway through when he began pondering what the hell possessed him to convince his family to visit the spook house on the outskirts of the county. They would have been better off going to the movies or to Taco Bell or—fuck it—simply staying home and doing jack squat. Jim doubted a heavy dose of psychedelics would make this particular haunted house worthwhile.

The thing was, the house was perfect for such an endeavor. It was old and creaky and quite a bit larger on the inside than what it appeared from the dirt parking lot. Wallpaper was tattered and floorboards were warped beyond belief. Yet there was an elegance to the place like it was a pretty nice abode back in whatever age it was crafted. The ceilings were high, baseboards and paneling were intricately carved, and certain doors and doorways came to a tall point at the top, rather than being flat like most doors.

While the house's original design offered cursory intrigue, the rest of it was horse shit. A better collection of Halloween decorations and scary costumes could be found at any Walmart on the planet. Spooky sounds were being emitted from crackling speakers in some of the rooms. Poorly constructed webs of cotton were everywhere, made even more ridiculous by the plastic tarantulas superglued throughout. A fog machine on its last leg sputtered from an open doorway, sending sad hills of fog crawling across the floorboards and dying between the cracks. Paper and cardboard cutouts of ghosts and vampires and witches were tacked to the walls in various spots, with no obvious rhyme or reason. The only thing offering even a hint of menace was the fake blood splattered all over the damn place like someone's five-year-old got a tad overzealous with the bucket of blood.

And the whole fucking place was drowning in orange lights.

If the decorations were bad, the experience itself was even worse. When the old man on the porch waved the Gibsons indoors, it was with no indication which direction to go or what exactly to do. Most haunted house attractions had a maze of sorts to follow. Some even had guides. Not this damn place. The family simply roamed room to room like they were exploring a random abandoned house on the side of the highway.

In each room, some idiot would jump out to greet them, either wearing a cheap plastic monster mask or a ghostly bedsheet. They would roar loudly and sufficiently make a fool of themselves before trotting down a hallway or into another room. In Jim's estimation, there weren't sufficient words to describe how poorly executed this haunted house was.

As he led the way through the foyer and living room and dining room—all of which still had furniture that looked original to the house, basically rotting into the floor with age—and then through a small empty room that could have once been a study, the buzzing warmth of opioid magic began coursing through him, yet Jim was becoming more bored and irritated by the second. If Mona had asked at that moment what he thought of the place, he would have told her he would much prefer being audited by the IRS while having his balls repeatedly smashed with a mallet. But she didn't ask so he didn't say so.

As they entered the next room, Maime said, "This is boring as fuck."

Rather than bemoan her daughter's language, Mona then said, "It's the Boones Farm of haunted houses, that's for sure."

As they crossed into a screened-in patio area, Julian pulled out his phone and began tapping away.

No one bothered stopping him.

Jim jiggled the handle on the patio's backdoor but it was locked. So he turned and led them through a second adjoining door back into the house. They walked quickly now, wanting simply to leave, passing more idiot monsters and clumsy ghosts. There was a paper werewolf tacked to the wall in one room—the only one of those Jim had seen. The orange glow was hurting his eyes and he thought he might clobber the next actor that yelled "Boo!" a little too close to his face.

They made their way through a kitchen and then a breakfast nook and finally back into the foyer that would lead them to the front porch where they'd begun. Only, there was a dead guy lying on the floor of the foyer now.

FOUR

He was dead and fat and nude. He was flayed open as if undergoing an autopsy, lying in a large, spreading pool of blood. His right arm had been chopped off just above the elbow; there was no sign of the rest of it. But Mona remembered the arm nailed to the tree at the entrance to the driveway. *Was it a right arm?*

There was the stench of rotting flesh in the room, and Mona wasn't sure if it was a new smell or one that had been here all along and was just stronger now. What she did know was that the swarm of flies was fresh to the scene. They hovered around the body like a cloud, many of them diving into the open chest and abdomen and meandering about on whatever organs she was seeing. The intestines—she recognized those for what they were—were drooped over the left side of the corpse, as if someone had reached in, pulled them out, and dropped them there beside the body, like it was for show, to provide a more graphic scene. If the intent was to shock and horrify, it worked.

Mamie was the first to scream, clutching her hands in front of her face and running into Julian on her way in a direction she was likely completely uncertain about.

Julian, whose eyes were like silver dollars, his phone held loosely in his hand somewhat forgotten, fell backward in utter shock from the collision. His back hit the floor with a *whap* and his precious phone went skittering.

Jim's stare wasn't leaving the corpse. His eyes bulged they were so wide. His mouth hung open and, if Mona's vision was relaying correctly in this weird orange light, a single string of drool was dripping from the corner of his mouth.

She watched all of this—the reactions of her family—with a pounding heartthrob in her ears. Her hands were clenched, the nails digging into her palms. She'd had a panic attack once, long ago before Julian was born, and her current frozen, witnessing state was very much like that, except so much worse. She felt like she couldn't breathe, like her heart was going to burst from her chest, like she may vomit at any moment.

"Jim," she managed to say through pursed lips, unsure if the word had even come out. Perhaps it was still stuck somewhere in her mind. Certainly no more words seemed intent on following her husband's name.

Suddenly, the front door burst open, causing Mona to jump and scream with a terror she hadn't felt since she was sixteen, all those years ago when she was—

"Surpriiiiiise!"

It was the old man, standing there with one hand on the brass door handle and the other holding his top hat, his white hair wild and wavering with the encroaching breeze. He smiled that hideous, yellow-orange smile.

Jim's head slowly corkscrewed in the old man's

direction, his mouth still ajar. Julian was propped up on his elbows now, eyes still on the body. Mamie had retreated to a dark corner of the adjoining room. Mona could hear her sobbing there.

"Bet y'all thought The Dark Side of Hell was horseshit 'til y'all saw that one," the old man said, his grin spreading further, his hand that was holding the doorknob now gesturing to the corpse on the floor.

"You mean?" Jim said, looking quickly back at the corpse.

"It's nothing but a gag, fella," the old man said, cackling. "Cost us a goddamn fortune though. You can bet your left nut on that."

Everyone looked back at the body and the surrounding flies. To Mona, it looked so fucking real. She'd seen plenty of horror movies with good practical effects, but this thing made her feel like she was in a butcher shop, not a slasher film. Hell, it even stunk of rot, like that time a mouse died beneath the kitchen sink, hidden behind several cleaners and dish rags and bug sprays. The whole kitchen smelled of rotting flesh until she'd found it and made Jim bag it up. Even after a thorough cleaning of the spot where the mouse's corpse melted away with rot beneath the sink, it still stunk for several days afterward. That stink—that stink and more— was in this room. Could it really be fake?

"Let's go," Jim said in a weak voice, looking around at his family. "Julian, get off the floor and let's go."

He waited until Julian, Mamie, and Mona were out the door before stepping out onto the porch, placing his hands on Mona's shoulders and squeezing. Was he being protective for once? Mona thought so.

The old man greeted them on the porch, smile wide as ever, his hat now back on his head, askew. He winked at Mona as she walked past but she gave him no mind, no reaction at all. Something about him wasn't right. He was sickly, not simply in a physical way. Something was really, *really* wrong with this man. She could see it in his eyes and in that smile.

"What did y'all think of our little spook house, Mr. Gibson?" the old man said, shifting his attention to Jim.

"It was, um, different," Jim said, and Mona looked back just in time to see him offer the old fart an uncomfortable smile.

"Different it is," the old man said, snapping his fingers as if this had been the greatest of compliments.

Mona looked toward the pumpkin patch as she descended the porch stairs behind her children. There was a scarecrow out there, roughly center of the patch. She hadn't noticed it before, and with the sun all but gone now, she couldn't make out the details at all. There were overalls and a sagging cowboy hat, that was for sure. And perhaps there was a face made of burlap, but maybe it was simply a face of straw. It looked creepy there amongst the pumpkins, like it grew there just like they did.

"Oh, I forgot!" the old man said, and now he came teetering to the edge of the porch, reaching inside his jacket with one hand, coming out with four slips of orange paper, each about the size of a bookmark. "You Gibsons, y'all have won the prize. Free passes to come on back here on Halloween!"

"Um," Jim said, reaching out slowly, taking the tickets, "thanks." He quickly stuffed them into his pocket and turned back to his family. "Let's go."

About halfway to the car, Mamie asked the question Mona already knew the answer to: "You're not seriously bringing us back out here on Halloween are you, Dad?"

"Fuck no," he said without hesitation.

"Jim, language," Mona said without much force. Her eyes drifted back to the pumpkin patch as they arrived at the car. She looked back at the scarecrow. It looked different somehow. Had it moved?

FIVE

"Fuck," Mamie said, sitting on a toilet seat with a loose screw in a stall in the girl's room, staring down at the second pregnancy test of the day. They'd both offered the same result.

It had been a week since the family's adventure at that creepy haunted house and two and a half months since Mamie had been on the rag. Two-plus goddamn months. She'd told that son-of-a-bitch to wear a rubber, but of course the passion of the moment took care of that idea.

Tucking the pregnancy test into her jacket pocket, Mamie then placed her face in her hands and her elbows on her knees and sobbed. This was the first time in ages she'd cried, perhaps the first time in five years. She was a tough girl, a hard cookie to crack. Some would look at her and think of her as goth and others may suggest emo. But Mamie didn't agree with either label. She was just Mamie, and she lived life to the beat of her own drum. To Hell with whatever anyone else thought.

She only cried for a moment, and then she took her black hair (dyed, of course), that had been draped around her weeping eyes, and tied it back in a tight ponytail. She wiped the drying tears away on her black denim sleeve. She took a deep breath and then pulled the scalpel from her other jacket pocket.

*

It was two months ago that she met Lance Bigsby at a party she wasn't supposed to attend. It was late August, summer still hanging on, and her best friend Raven thought it would be a swell time for a party at her parent's beachfront cabin.

Neither the beachfront nor the cabin were as glamorous as those words alone lent a mind to believe. The beach was more mud than sand, a black, sticky mud at that. The lake in which it was situated was more of a large, glorified pond, little more than eight acres in overall size. And the cabin, it was literally that—a cabin like one might expect to find in an old film about trappers in Colorado or gold miners in California or Alaska. It was a no-bullshit cabin, free of electricity and made of logs. Raven's dad and uncle had been the builders some fifteen or twenty years ago.

It was a muggy day at this beachfront cabin in North Texas, and at first Mamie wished she hadn't come. She wasn't a fan of crowds *or* the outdoors, and while she did enjoy checking out various insects when she came across them, the threat of late-summer snakes was enough to keep her from digging around too deep for any creepy crawlies.

"What's the matter with you?" Raven had said on

this day, sitting in a crudely made rocking chair on what passed as the cabin's porch. She was smoking a cigarette and had a Miller Lite in her hand, its surface wet and dripping.

"It's just hot," Mamie said, standing several yards in front of Raven and several yards away from where the yellowing grass gave way to the muddy beach. "Plus, there's not shit to do out here, Rave. I told you that before."

"Oh," Raven said, smiling now, "I fixed that for you, darling. There's going to be plenty to do here soon."

"What do you mean by that? If you're talking about performing a satanic ritual, I'm totally in. But if you invited a bunch of people out here for a party, count me out."

Raven laughed, spitting out a swallow of beer. "You'll have fun, Mamie. You'll love it."

"Fuck you, you invited a bunch of people out here? Not my cup of tea and fucking know it, Rave!" She turned away from her friend, taking a few steps toward the lake, just shy of getting her black Doc Martens muddy on the beach. She crossed her arms and stared at the gently rippling water. "I can't believe you drug me out here for a party. Who the hell is coming?"

"Chill out, chick," Raven said, standing up and sucking on her cigarette and tossing it in the grass before taking a quick sip of beer. "Just a few people. Ami and Beth and Derek. Some friend of his."

"A friend? Who?" Mamie said, spinning around. She was no fan of Derek, a hog for attention if there ever was one. She knew he and Raven had slept together on a number of occasions but that didn't mean *she* had to enjoy his pompous company.

"I don't know," Raven said, shrugging. "Lance

something, I think. He's from out of town somewhere. But here's the good part, Mamie darling: they're bringing weed. And alcohol, of course. Lots of it!"

And they had. They'd also brought a good many more guests than Raven suggested when it was just the two of them. It was a party the likes of which hadn't been seen at that muddy little cabin since Raven's dad threw a shindig upon its completed construction. The cabin and beach and the surrounding woods were covered in rowdy teenagers, most of whom were puffing on joints and chugging far more beer than their teen bodies should consume.

One of those teen bodies was a sandy-haired, blue-eyed boy named Lance Bigsby. Mamie was instantly struck by his handsome looks and equally struck by what he wore—a black Slayer t-shirt and tattered black jeans that fit him perfectly. He looked like a boy that belonged in a colored shirt and khaki shorts, and the awkwardness of his charming face and strong body in his grungy black attire made him all the more desirable to Mamie. This was a boy in revolt against who he was brought up to be, a boy who didn't believe in the status quo, a boy who would understand her.

In reality, he understood her just enough to convince her to drop her panties. By the time Mamie discovered his wardrobe was specifically picked out by Raven so Lance would have a better chance of bedding down with her, the deed had already been done. He got his dick wet and Mamie was played for a fool.

*

Now here she sat on a high school girl's room toilet with a scalpel to her wrist and a baby growing in her belly.

Was it considered a murder-suicide if a pregnant girl killed herself? She didn't know. Dad would probably say yes. Mom might say no.

She'd done the first test before school, at home with Mom ranting about her and Julian being late if they didn't 'hurry the hell up.' With her nerves causing her to quake uncontrollably during second period Biology, she asked to be excused and ran to the restroom to test it again, praying to whatever god there was that the first one had been a false positive.

Just in case that wasn't the case, Mamie snatched the scalpel off her desk as she went. It was frog dissection day, so scalpels were aplenty. Truth be told, she was kind of looking forward to slicing open the frog and digging through its organs. Instead, it would be her wrist. No way was she having a baby. No way was she listening to Mom and Dad berate her and call her a whore and tell her she'd fucked up her entire life. No way was she getting an abortion either. The same madness would ensue whether she killed the baby or kept it. And if she tried to hanger the fucker out of her cunt herself? Yeah, a better way to die was by the knife. Mamie wasn't afraid of the darkness. It was *life* she didn't much care for. It was her parents who didn't understand her, who she would happily stroll into the void to get away from.

Fuck it, she thought, placing the razor edge of the scalpel to her wrist, right where the artery should be, assuming the anatomy charts were right. She began to apply pressure, and the tiniest glint of blood was forming around the steel, when she heard the gunshot.

SIX

Mona Lisa Gibson was her real name, at least since her days as a single lady with the maiden name Belincort. She was timid in her daily life, preferring to stay home for a good movie over going out to do much of anything. Most of her extended family was dead and buried, and there were only a handful of ladies around Mangle County she considered friends, and only in the loosest sense of the word. In reality, there was no one she was terribly close to, no friendship worthy of her most intimate thoughts and feelings.

Indeed, Mona was known far less around town than she was online. She was known far and wide on the ol' interwebs. Her tax papers listed her occupation as a "content creator," which wasn't altogether false; she was a cam girl, going by the name Daisy Plays.

It wasn't what she grew up wanting to be down the road in Mark's Point, of course. No child grows up wanting to shake their ass for cash from drooling, undesirable old men. Though, she reckoned that may not be altogether true anymore, in the age of viral TikTok booty-shakin'. Like most kids, Mona grew up bouncing back and forth between what she wanted to do in her adulthood. She wanted to be a ballerina, of course, and a teacher and a nurse and a veterinarian, all the stuff little girls typically aspire to do. Most of all, though, she wanted to be a fisherman, like her dad.

Mark's Point was a small relatively poor community on a crooked finger-like peninsula jutting out into Lake Spirit, and Mona's dad was a catfishing guide there. He didn't bring his family back much money but he sure brought back the stories. Yes, like fishermen far and wide, he brought back the stories. The more far-fetched the better. He would tell tales of fighting massive catfish or alligator gar or carp. He would boast about how his clients could hardly believe the size of the fish he brought in. Typically, he conveniently didn't have his Polaroid handy when they got the fish reeled in. Mona knew, most times, what this meant. He was fibbing a little bit but probably just a little, and she was okay with that. Her favorite fables of the lake were those of the supernatural ilk. Her dad, on several occasions, told of a mysterious tentacled creature below the surface of Lake Spirit. He talked about ghosts in the nearby woods. He talked about deadly animals not far away, near Stagsville, called draggers; they supposedly dragged their unwitting victims through trees and brush before killing them. Those were Mona's favorite stories.

But what she liked more than anything was going fishing with her dad. He never took her when he had clients, so she didn't get to go as often as she would have liked. But two or three times a month, she could talk him into an evening on the lake in his five-seater motorboat.

Those days, even now, were the best of her life.

It was too bad those times would be tainted by rape when she was sixteen.

*

They would expect a special show on Halloween, this much Mona knew. So she'd prepared, buying matching orange lace bra and thong panties. She'd painted her fingernails orange with black polka dots. She painted her lips black and made her eyeshadow extra dark. And, with a touch she actually quite liked, she added a witch's hat and broom.

She went live every Tuesday and Thursday morning, with the occasional Saturday night gig when a special holiday or birthday was coming up, or when the summer heat gave the Gibsons an extra hefty electric bill. With Christmas not far in the future, Mona knew a Daisy Plays Saturday Night Special would likely be in her future too. She would have to send the kids to stay with friends and she'd probably be stuck with Jim watching from the corner and giving his pecker the ol' one-two, but it would bring in a ton of cash, as always.

Also, as always, the Saturday Night Special would bring out the freaks. She didn't exactly enjoy herself even on Tuesdays and Thursdays, despite actually achieving orgasm on occasion, but Saturdays . . . they were grueling.

"stick the biggest dildo you have in your ass"

"Put a toothbrush in yo pussy then brush yo teeth wit it"

"deep throat the cucumber till you vomit"

"then lick it up"

"You do scat stuff?"

"Pee in a glass of ice for daddy..."

"How much for body mutilation?"

It got pretty fuckin' wild on Saturdays, when the viewership was large, and many of them were dosed-up on their weekend drug or drink of choice. She turned down a lot of money on those nights, not willing to go where many of them desired. That ticked Jim off sometimes, that she would turn down a thousand bucks or more to drink a glass of her own piss, but she sure as fuck didn't see him volunteering to do it. Anyway, she did plenty of sick shit she didn't really *want* to do, all in the name of a decent payday.

So, hopefully, Halloween morning, a Tuesday this year, would be like her typical weekday shows, with six or seven horny losers logging in to watch her dance around and finger herself, with maybe a little dildo or vibrator action if they wanted to throw her a few extra bucks. But no big bucks with big demands.

Mona prepared her filming room—the spare bedroom any time the kids were home, with the camera and sex toys and any props stored neatly away in the closet—by situating some orange and black pillows on the bed and dangling silly paper spiders from the ceiling, positioning them so they'd just barely be in the picture.

As she was hanging these, just for a second, she thought of The Dark Side of Hell, about the cheap decorations they had there. Until the end, at least. Mona had nightmares for three nights following that experience. She still found it difficult to get the image of that corpse— supposedly fake—out of her mind. Because of this, her Thursday performance lacked enthusiasm and the incoming dollars proved this. But the thought of it was almost gone from her mind now. Almost.

Mona placed a handful of sex toys on the bed, most of them orange or black or lime green in the spirit of the season. One of them was a big green tentacle, perfect for Halloween, but it would take at least a fifty spot for her to use that one.

Glancing in the mirror across from the bed and behind the iPad camera, she looked at herself, adjusting the witch hat, pulling one side of her bra up just a hair. She was nearing forty now but still looked pretty good, in her opinion. Her butt was round and her tits weren't quite to the point of needing a lift and her blonde hair only had the occasional gray. But all that was coming. Smiling weakly at herself, Mona moved over to the iPad, checking the time then turning on the live feed.

"Fuck," she whispered almost instantly, too quiet for the viewers to hear, hopefully. There were already nineteen viewers logged in to watch. And the absurd requests were already rolling in.

*

"Happy Halloween!" Mona exclaimed, waving two hands at her audience and smiling broadly as she sat back onto the bed atop the witch's broom she'd placed there. It was a prop broom, made of bound sticks and straw, and she wrapped her legs beneath the shaft and gripped it with two hands like a giant cock. "Looks like we have a lot of viewers on this spooky morning!" She bit her lip seductively. "Who's ready to have some fun?"

"Shove dat broom up dat pussy!"

She ignored that one, among others.

"You are such lovely women hope make you wife"

Though this was a ridiculous comment, Mona reached for the iPad screen and hearted the comment. Sometimes the creeps wanting love paid the best. The comments continued rolling in, most calling her sexy or beautiful or commenting on her Halloween attire. Within the first thirty seconds of the stream, another dozen viewers had logged in.

"Mmm, I love seeing so many of my naughty friends on this spooky Halloween morning," she said, biting her lip, spreading her legs apart and letting her right hand glide gently over the top of her orange panties. "The more people watching, the better. I love when lots of people watch me fuck myself."

Mona then heard the whir of a lawnmower next door. It wasn't uncommon in North Texas to be mowing one's lawn all the way into late December, and now the neighbor apparently thought it was a good time to do just that. Mona sighed. She considered complaining about the mower to her audience, but that would take their minds, however briefly, away from her tits and pussy—the money-makers.

"Stick that tentacle dildo in your pussy!"

"Maybe y'all would like to see my pretty pink nipples first," Mona said, cringing as the mower grew louder. Her neighbor (either Harold or his wife Tilly) was mowing on *this* side of the yard, closest to the Gibson house. She was certain her viewers could hear it whirring now.

-$150-

The donation popped up on her end of the screen in green bold font. Then:

"Tentacle in pussy! Please!"

"Well, you know what you want, don't you?" Mona said seductively, a fake voice she had learned to turn off and on in an instant. "Coming right up. Or should I say *cumming* right up?" She giggled, covering her mouth with a hand. "Let me just grab my lube."

Taking the broom from beneath her and sliding to the

edge of the bed, she slid the nightstand's drawer open and pulled out a small bottle of KY. She looked at the camera and smiled, showing her audience the bottle, waggling it at them. Just then, the doorbell rang.

Mona scrunched her nose and grimaced. They had a clear *No Solicitors!* sign on their front door, but this wasn't the first time her doorbell had rang in the middle of her performance. On the couple of other times, she'd ignored it and the ring hadn't come a second time.

"Whoever is at the door," she said, leaning in close to the camera, "they're just gonna have to come back another time. Daisy Plays is all yours. And this big tentacle dildo is all mine!"

But as she slid back toward the middle of the bed, reaching for the dildo, the doorbell rang again. And then again. And again. It rang repeatedly several times, so quickly that the ring wasn't allowed to complete fully.

"What the fuck?" Mona said under her breath. She held a finger up to her audience. "Hold on, my sexy lovelies, some idiot is playing games."

Sliding off the end of the bed and walking beyond view of the camera, she reached the bedroom window and pulled down one of the closed blinds, peering out toward the street. This window faced the neighbor's house, but she hoped if she leaned close to the window, she could see a car she recognized out front. Instead, she saw her middle-aged neighbor Tilly mowing in a tank-top and shorts, walking toward their connecting backyards. As she passed by the window, the older woman saw Mona's eyes in the window and smiled at her, nodding.

Mona didn't respond, though later she regretted that. Because walking behind Tilly was a man dressed in all black except for the bright orange, plastic jack-o'-lantern mask covering his face. He was walking quickly, right on her heels. He too looked at Mona in the window, cocking his head and waving at her. Then, as Mona crinkled her brow in confusion, the man pulled a large Glock pistol from a holster at his side and, before Mona had a second to respond, blew a hole in the back of Tilly's head, a bright red cloud bursting out the front of her face, her body slumping over the mower at first, then falling to the side, her gaping skull staring blankly at the window as it came to rest as if staring straight at Mona.

When Mona finally screamed, the bedroom door behind her burst open.

*

As Mona spun around, already screaming, she was confronted by two men in black coveralls rushing at her— each of them were wearing identical plastic pumpkin masks as the murderer outside the window.

The man reaching her first grabbed Mona tight by the arms and flung her to the bed, her skull rapping hard on the headboard, leaving her momentarily dazed and seeing stars. The man jumped on the bed after her, straddling Mona and pinning her down, holding her wrists as tears escaped her eyes and screams escaped her mouth. The other man, who was huge, hovered at the bedside, clutching a crowbar in one hand and, as Mona turned her head and witnessed through bleary eyes, what appeared to be a rolled-up baby's diaper.

"Are we live?" the man atop her said, his voice sounding awkwardly like it was coming from an old radio beneath the plastic mask. But Mona's mind was wild with fear and confusion, so she didn't respond. The man looked toward the iPad then back at Mona then at the iPad again. Comments and numbers were popping up with haste, and new viewers were flooding in. "Yeah, we fuckin' live, baby!"

"double team her! DP!"

-$40-

-$10-

-$200-

"Hell yeah! Rape that bitch!"

"Fuck her wit da crowbar"

-$25-

-$88-

"I pay for tentacle fuck but dis fine... I guess"

-$100-

"What's with the fuckin diaper?"

The man on top of Mona started laughing, then he looked down at her. She could see that the skin around his eyes was painted black beneath the mask, and the eyes, though shadowed, were light green and mean. He shook her wrists and leaned down close to her face.

"They want to know what's up with the diaper," he said, and Mona could hear the evil smile in his words.

"Please, let me go," she said, another tear falling. "I promise, I w—"

"Won't tell anyone?" the man said, cocking his head. "Yeah, we've heard that bullshit before." He straightened himself up atop her, then turned toward the camera. "So, y'all want to see what the diaper is all about, huh?"

"Yes"

-$250-

"duh"

"yes"

"yyyyyyyeeeeesssss!!!!!"

"YES"

-$75-

"Yes! Yes! Yes!"

"You folks are gonna love this. This will be top-notch jerking your chicken material." He turned back toward Mona, looking down on her with those evil green eyes, his hands tightening on her wrists. "You want to know what's in the diaper, Mrs. Gibson?"

"Please, just let me go," she said, more tears streaming. But it occurred to her that this man used her last name, like he knew exactly who she was, like all this was planned ahead of time, like she was picked specifically.

"Oh, excuse me," the man said, shrugging his shoulders as if he'd made a mistake. "Not Mrs. Gibson, but Ms. Plays, right? Daisy Plays, do you want to know what's in the baby diaper there?" He nodded to the other man, who wiggled it in his gloved hand.

"Please..."

"You see," he said, turning his masked face once more to the camera, "we kidnapped this old hag from behind a nursing home, oh, about a year ago. The Dalmatian House, maybe you heard of it. This old, fat bitch was sitting in a wheelchair on the back porch of the place, smoking a cigarette. Well, we drove by and snatched her fat ass up and chucked her in the van, just like we're gonna do Daisy Plays here."

"No, please," Mona whimpered.

"When we got her to the house, we slapped her around and stripped her down and everything. Muk was about to peel her loose skin off with a pair of pliers and fry it when he noticed the funk wafting up from that bitch's loins. Turns out she had some sort of infection of the snatch. Smelled like cheese down there, and that cooch of hers dripped with some sort of slimy sludge. It was Plastic Monster's idea that we not kill her." The man nodded at the one holding the diaper and crowbar. "Said we should fuck that sloppy cunt of hers. So, that's what we done. We all had our way with her. The wet, smacking sound that cooch of her made...and that smell, goddamn. Ol' Muk never did get to skin her; we kept her alive for that rotten-ass pussy. Was too good to just toss away, you know."

Mona could feel the slickness of sweat on her wrists, beneath the man's grip. Unlike his companion, this man atop her was gloveless, and the sweat between their flesh might provide just enough lubrication for her to slip away, bucking him off at the same time. She would have to deal with the other guy too, of course, this Plastic Monster or whatever he was called, wielding his crowbar and a diaper that somehow had something to do with raping an elderly woman. The witch broom was beside her, having slid to the edge of the bed, wedged between the mattress and the wall, right beside an orange double-ended dildo. She would have to grab the broom to defend herself. She would need to hit them both and hit them hard. If she let herself be kidnapped, Mona was as good as dead.

"Now," the man continued, "you wouldn't think an old bitch like that would have workin' parts. But she did. That belly of hers started swelling and several months down the line she spit a baby out of her rank twat, ruining my favorite rug in the process." He huffed, shaking his head, looking down at Mona then back to the camera.

"There's something wrong with that goddamn baby, let me tell ya'. Deformed and stupid. Never cries though. Just looks at you, drooling. And it's got some kind of disease—a disease of the gut. No matter what you feed that little bastard, its shit comes out...well, about the thickness of tomato sauce, except it's brown of course. And, goddamn, it's the worst smelling, most foul substance on the Earth. Nothing—and I mean nothing—

smells worse than that mutant baby's shit."

The man's sweaty grip had loosened a tad while telling this disgusting story. Mona clinched her fists, ready to throw punches as needed, and prepared her hips to buck the man off as best she could. She would yell at her audience while doing this, telling them to call 911, screaming her address to them, information she couldn't imagine herself divulging to her loyal group of perverts under any other situation.

"Go ahead, Plastic," the man said.

Before Mona could make her move, the Plastic Monster fella unwrapped the diaper, opening it wide, the sour, rotten smell instantly filling the air, and shoved it into Mona's face with a splat. She screamed as shit seeped into her nose and mouth, the man's hand keeping the diaper pressed firmly against her. The man on top of her was right—it was without question the worst smell she'd ever encountered, like if decaying flesh, bad fish, and rotten milk were all one odor. She sucked it in as she breathed and screamed, gurgling on its bitter taste.

Mona slipped from the man's grasp, swinging her fists wildly, blindly. The diaper fell away, but shit remained painted across her face as she thrust her body upward, trying to buck the man off. But he didn't go easily, his legs tightening on her waist. Mona's eyes fluttered open, searching for weapons, but the shit caked along her eyelids left her vision blurred.

"Stay still, bitch!" the man yelled. "You ain't getting away!"

She reached to the edge of the bed, finding the double-ended dildo. Grabbing it, she swung, feeling it collide with the man's face.

"Goddammit! Plastic Monster, help me out here!"

Mona bucked again, and this time the man partially

fell away. She struggled up to her elbows, pulling one of her legs up to deliver a powerful kick. But as she looked over at Plastic Monster, seeing through her blurred vision that he still held the dripping diaper in one hand, she saw the crowbar coming at her head.

Just before everything went black, Mona heard the man speak once more.

"Damn, Daisy Plays is making a shit ton of money today. Too bad your dead ass won't be able to spend it."

SEVEN

"I told you to be here at eight, Jimmy."

Norton Irish had a face and frame that fit his husky voice perfectly. Sitting behind the polished mahogany desk, clear of any clutter aside from a few expensive-looking pens and a spiral notepad, was a man who should have been a linebacker for the Cowboys in his younger years. He was tall and wide, though not fat, and Jim was certain the maroon blazer Norton wore had been custom-made to fit such a large body. Beneath the jacket, he wore a beige turtleneck, a garment Norton wore no matter the season, even with the inferno-like summers Texas typically delivered. Jim thought this touch made him look like a villain from a James Bond film. Norton's face didn't help dispel this notion: the flesh there was pockmarked and beefy, and a light-colored scar ran from the left corner of his mouth all the way across his cheek, ending just an inch from his earlobe. (Rumor had it, this blemish was from a street fight in Chicago, when a lowlife drug addict attacked Norton with a switchblade in an attempt to lift the coke he hadn't the money to buy; rumor also had it Norton, with his cheek flayed open, used the same switchblade to cut off the druggy's head, which he then hand-delivered to the guy's mother.) He had wavy red hair, graying at the temples, slicked straight back, and like his turtlenecks, he always wore brown sunglasses, whether indoors or out, day or night.

"I said," Norton repeated, "I told you to be here at eight."

"I know it, Nort," Jim said, smiling nervously and shrugging. "Look—"

"Don't call me Nort, Jimmy. My friends call me Nort. You are not my friend. You call me Mr. Irish. Got it?"

"Right, sorry about that, uh, Mr. Irish." Jim moved to sit in one of the two leather chairs stationed before Norton's desk.

"Don't fuckin' sit down neither," Norton said, then looked to his left. "You believe this guy? Comes in here acting like he owns the place."

Standing to Norton's left, leaned against a bookcase of bound leather books and smoking a cigarette, was Antonio Lugosi, Norton's righthand man. He was slender and shorter than average, with dark hair and eyes, his suit equally dark. Jim had no doubt there was a gun hidden in that suit somewhere, loaded and chambered, ready for action. Antonio was shaking his head, his eyes locked on Jim.

He swallowed, sweat creeping up on his forehead. He clasped his hands in front of him, not sure what to do or say. He knew *why* he'd been summoned. But were they going to kill him for it? Surely not.

"I also told you to come alone. Who the fuck is the

broad in your Mercedes?"

Jim cleared his throat then said, "Um, that's my nurse. Sherry."

"Sherry, huh? She don't have her own goddamn car?"

"It's in the shop. I'm giving her a ride to work." This was a lie. In reality, he'd brought Sherry along just in case, on the off chance, shit went sideways. If they planned on killing him, they might think twice with a witness in the car outside.

Norton looked at his watch, a gold Rolex. "Your office opens at nine, Jimmy. It's just after ten. You were supposed to be here at fuckin' eight and now you've magically arrived two hours late with your fuckin' nurse in the car. Who the hell is at your office taking care of patients?"

"Um, Myra, my secretary," Jim said, forcing a small smile. "She's there."

"Boy," Norton said, shaking his head, "you're some kind of fuckin' doctor. Leaving your patients to fuckin' wait while you do fuck knows what. You fuckin' that nurse, Jimmy, that fuckin' Sherry chick? You fuckin' her?"

"Um…" Jim said, swallowing hard again. What did this have to do with anything?

"I thought so. You're a piece of work, Jimmy, a real piece of work. You believe this guy, Tony?"

"He's a dirtbag," Antonio said, smiling wryly at Jim.

"A goddamn dirtbag. And I helped you out, Jimmy. I helped you out and you fuckin' spit on me by showing up late when I call on you."

"I'm sorry about that, Nor—um, Mr. Irish." He looked down at his feet, nervously.

"Look at me, goddammit!"

Jim did. Norton's face had twisted into a scowl beneath those shades, veins popping out at the temples.

"Why ain't you been writing the prescriptions like you used to, huh? I send my boys to your office and you're sending them back with scripts for fuckin' Motrin and Epsom salt. You lost your goddamn mind, Jimmy? I ain't fuckin' selling Motrin and Epsom salt."

"I know, Mr. Irish," Jim said, holding up his hands in a defensive manner. "But look, the feds are cracking down on opioids. These aren't the pill mill days. I can't write twenty scripts a day for twenty-milligram Norco, especially in a small town like Twin Oaks. There's only two pharmacies; they'll notice shit like that. My license would be—"

"Your license? Jimmy, if it weren't for me you wouldn't have a license to be concerned about. If it weren't for me, you'd be in jail, isn't that right?"

"Yes, but—"

"You came to me, Jimmy. I didn't come to you. You were nothin' but a doped-up doctor with half a dozen malpractice suits and an accidental death on his hands when I met you. I didn't *need* shit from you, Jimmy. But I helped you out because I'm a small-town guy. I do most my business in Dallas and Houston, but Twin Oaks is my home. We take care of each other here. And I took care of your problems, didn't I?"

Jim looked down at his feet, then back up at Norton before he had a chance to chastise him for looking away.

"I made your problems disappear. I made two fuckin' people disappear, Jimmy." Norton held up two fingers, emphasizing this. "And did you have to give me any money for that courtesy?"

"No," Jim muttered, lips pursed.

"What's that you say, Jim? Speak up."

"No, I didn't have to pay you, Mr. Irish."

"That's right. You didn't have to sell your Mercedes or take out a second mortgage or any shit like that. Just write some prescriptions when I send you patients. That's all I asked. It ain't fuckin' hard."

"I know, but you're sending so many—"

"I don't give a fuck!" Norton yelled, pointing at Jim. "If I send you a hundred fellas a day, you write a hundred fuckin' scripts for what they ask for! If you don't—by god, Jimmy—you'll be disappearing next. This is my business." He tapped a thumb against his broad chest. "It's hard enough I got to compete against these fuckin' Mexican cartels, without some pencil dick doctor not doing the job he's supposed to fuckin' do. When I send you a patient, you give him what the fuck he asks for. Got that?"

"Yes," Jim said, resisting the need to wipe sweat from his brow. "Yes, Mr. Irish."

"Good," Norton said, then turned to Antonio. "Tony, walk this prick to his car."

"You got it," Antonio said, sucking on his cigarette and making for the door. "Follow me, Doc."

Wordlessly, Jim turned to follow. As he passed through the door of Norton's office, he heard the man's voice once more.

"And Jimmy—"

Jim turned around, slowly, waiting for a bullet or a knife to the gut from Antonio.

"Happy Halloween."

*

"Thanks for the escort, Antonio," Jim said, giving Norton's minion a fake bow as they arrived at his

Mercedes.

"Don't make me call after you again, Doc," Antonio said as Jim opened the door of his still-running car, sliding into the driver seat. Antonio, holding the door open, leaned down and looked across Jim at Sherry. "Hi there," he said, nodding to the woman, his eyes locking on her, no doubt memorizing her features. Then Antonio closed the door gently and gave Jim a thumbs up through the window.

"What was that about?" Sherry asked, taking a break from applying her makeup to talk.

"Don't worry about it," Jim said, checking the rearview mirror and throwing the car in reverse, backing out of the parking space right in front of the pawnshop that covered for Norton's headquarters. "We gotta get to the office."

"No shit, Sherlock," Sherry said. "We're late for three appointments. One of them is that Henderson kid with the spinal injury. He has a sore throat and headache. Myra has texted me four times asking where we're at."

"Maybe if you hadn't insisted on fucking before we left your house then we wouldn't be late." Jim looked over at her as he pulled into the street, heading north in the direction of downtown Twin Oaks, where his office was. Sherry glared at him.

"Excuse me, I did not insist," she said. "Besides, you're the one that stopped at a pawnshop for some goddamn reason. Like you need any more debt, Dr. Gibson." She chuckled, shaking her head as she looked at the mirror in her compact.

"My finances are none of your damn business," Jim snapped, his hands gripping the steering wheel much as they did the night he took his family to the spook house. "You wouldn't know what it's like taking care of a family while also paying off school loans and malpractice lawyers for bullshit lawsuits. You have no fucking clue, Sherry. You live with a fucking cat. You have no responsibilities."

"Oh sure," Sherry said, applying powder to her cheeks, "bullshit lawsuits. I guess nicking someone's artery during a standard suture procedure, because you were fuckin' high on coke, is one of those bullshit lawsuits. Also, don't forget how you lost ten grand gambling on football two weeks ago." She laughed again, not a real laugh but one meant to irritate Jim, which it did.

"It's none of your fucking business, Sherry," he said, not looking at her but pointing a finger in her direction.

"Oh, I know," she said, smiling. "I almost feel bad for that bitch wife of yours. Your financial troubles must really stress her out. You must be the only doctor in Texas who can't pay his fuckin' bills."

"Shut up about it, Sherry," Jim said, gritting his teeth, seething. He'd taken enough shit from Norton Irish; he didn't need more shit from his fucking nurse/fuck buddy.

"It'll be my problem though if my paycheck ever bounces. That wouldn't be good, Dr. Gibson."

Jim looked over at her, his head pulsing with anger. She was smiling at him, devilishly. What the fuck was she getting at? He'd never failed to pay her, *or* Myra, throughout all his financial troubles.

"I was just thinking, it's probably about time I got a raise." She grinned and shrugged then tucked her makeup shit back into her purse.

"The fuck are you talking about?" Jim said, practically feeling the steam spewing from his ears. "You're a goddamn LVN, and you're making more than most RNs."

"I know it," Sherry said, sounding all bubbly. "But I don't want the things I know accidentally slipping out. You know what I mean, Dr. Gibson? A little extra pay may help me remember not to tell anyone about your infidelities. Not just with me. But Myra and the pharmacy lady and that patient who is only seventeen that comes in every other week, just to see you. I don't want to accidentally tell anyone about that."

The road was a blur. Jim looked at Sherry, seeing her smiling, conniving face, her pearly white teeth staring back at him, teeth he'd paid to have fixed. He imagined himself stopping the car, slamming it in park, then wrapping his hands around Sherry's neck, choking her until there was no life left in her eyes, choking her until that stupid smile of hers was guaranteed to never return. It had been a major mistake taking *her* to bed. Jim had made plenty mistakes over the years, but this fucking bitch took the cake. Yet, if she were to offer up some pussy right this second, he knew he would relent. Jim had his crutches—booze, drugs, gambling—but good pussy was the mother of all crutches, and Sherry damn well knew it.

"I'll give it some thought," Jim said as they pulled up to a stop sign. He stared straight ahead, not wanting to look in Sherry's direction. Three more blocks and they would reach his office, where he was boss without question. He would put Sherry and Myra to work and try to forget all his problems, for at least a few hours.

"Don't think on it too long, deary," Sherry said, and Jim could hear her pull her compact back out, as if she needed to inspect her appearance for the fiftieth time in the last five minutes.

Letting out a long sigh, Jim pulled forward, easing past the stop sign and into the intersection, at the same time reaching into the center console with his right hand, grabbing a pre-filled miniature ziplock baggy of the Holy Trinity—a medication combo of Oxycontin, Soma, and Xanax. There had been no other cars at the four-way stop, so he'd pulled away from his stop with barely a glance at the road he was crossing, simultaneously dumping the three pills from its baggy into his mouth, crunching and swallowing them away. It was far too late when he finally saw the black van bearing down on them from his right at 50mph or more, with no apparent desire to stop at the stop sign.

*

The collision seemed to happen in slow motion. Jim's head turned to watch, his eyes going wide with shock as the van smashed directly into the passenger door. Sherry hadn't seen it coming, her mind far away again, staring into the compact until the final split second. Jim yelled out an unrecognizable curse with the full force of the van rocking him to the side, the passenger windows shattering inward, much of the glass slicing through Sherry's flesh, ripping her face to shreds. The windshield spiderwebbed and buckled, but didn't break completely. The Mercedes skittered sideways, losing its forward momentum completely. Jim's head cracked against his window, bringing forth an instant throbbing headache, followed by sharp pains in his right arm and leg.

His world went blurry and dazed, his foot coming off the gas. When his eyes cleared, pain increasing by the second, Jim thought he'd perhaps passed out and came back to fifteen or twenty minutes later, for he felt as if he'd taken a long agonizing nap. In reality, he'd only been out a few seconds.

Looking over at Sherry, he saw the skin of her face hanging in bloody ribbons, soaking her green scrubs red. But that wasn't the worst of it; her face could be fixed by a good surgeon. But her right leg and arm—they would require a good deal more work, assuming she survived. Her femur was clearly shattered, with the lower half of the large leg bone jutting out of her inner thigh, blood pouring from around it. Her right forearm—perhaps it had been resting on the door at the time of collision—was as deformed as any traumatic injury Jim had ever seen. The once smooth, toned forearm was now lumpy with breaks, the extremity zigzaging in all different directions. She gurgled a weak noise, a moan of pain.

As Jim reached for her with his right hand, it too bloodied from exploded glass, his door was yanked open, and he found himself tumbling backward, spilling into the street, hitting his head once more on the rough asphalt.

"Fuck, you're not helping!" he yelled out, reaching for his pounding noggin, squinting at a sky that was too bright.

Then it occurred to him: he was being taken out. Norton Irish had had his fill of dealing with Dr. Jim Gibson. He didn't kill him at the office because he didn't want to bloody up his rugs. Or maybe he wanted to wait until they knew for sure who was in the car. That's why Antonio Lugosi followed him all the way to the car, staring in at Sherry as he bid them farewell. A farewell indeed. They were being knocked off in broad daylight in little ol' Twin Oaks.

He opened his eyes, not yet accepting his fate but wanting to stare death in the eyes, wanting to see the bullet or blade that came next. But what he saw was an orange jack-o'-lantern mask, made of plastic and reflecting the early sunlight. The pumpkin tilted its head as if inspecting Jim, marveling at him perhaps.

And then dark hands were on him, lifting him violently off the ground. Jim winced and yelled out in pain. He was taken up by two pair of hands, his feet dragging across the pavement toward—yes, toward the black van, its front end with barely a blemish from the wreck.

As he went, seemingly too tired to fight back, Jim saw what appeared to be an old lady with a pumpkin mask, her curly white hair a mess in the wind. She was dressed all in black like his captors, and she was leaning into Jim's Mercedes, leaning across the driver seat, her back audibly creaking, stabbing Sherry repeatedly in the chest and gut with a long hunting knife.

EIGHT

It was too early still.

Julian was thinking 10:22am would be perfect. He was born at 10:22am, if his birth certificate was to be believed. Today, he would be born again at that very same time.

Twenty-three minutes away then.

Mr. Scofield was talking about Hemingway, about *For Whom the Bell Tolls,* talking as if he knew Robert Jordan personally. He kept mispronouncing several of the names, including Pilar, which wasn't a difficult name at all, in Julian's opinion. He kept looking down at his iPad there on the podium, stealing the thoughts of others for his lectures. Mr. Scofield didn't know anything beyond what he read on Wikipedia.

Julian was in the ninth grade, a freshman, a grade ahead of where he should be at thirteen. He wouldn't be driving age until the spring semester of his junior year of high school. That, of course, assumed he'd still be going to school at Twin Oaks High in two years.

He wouldn't be.

Not after today.

Billie Standifer was the most popular girl in the freshman class. She sat on the front row in the middle. Her curly blonde hair was up in a ponytail, showing off her long neck and dangling earrings. She made straight A's. She was a cheerleader and a soccer player, so she had nice thighs, full and muscular. Nice rearend too, or so Julian heard from the boys who gave a shit.

He *did not* give a shit.

Not because he was gay or anything like that.

He detested boys as much as girls.

Billie Standifer, so it was rumored, had sex with her soccer coach, Coach Madsen, a woman. Julian didn't much believe that rumor but it mattered little. From his position near the back of the room, he could see that she wore leather sandals to school today, with a silver anklet dangling a single charm—the letter P. Julian wondered what the P signified. He supposed he'd never know. He imagined sawing Billie's legs off with a bow saw.

This thought aroused Julian.

At the front right corner of the classroom's seated students was George Lim, whose parents emigrated from China, naming their only son after George Washington. George Lim wore glasses and talked with a lisp and wore pleated slacks and always asked way too many questions.

Julian had a locker next to George two years ago, and George tried multiple times to strike up a friendship. He invited Julian over to his house to play Fortnite. He invited Julian to his birthday party at Mazzio's Pizza. He tried to talk Julian into joining the chess club.

Julian didn't want friends, however.

George's mother died of pancreatic cancer.

After her death, George said to Julian, almost off-handedly, that he didn't miss his mother.

That was the only time Julian ever wanted to talk to George, to press him for further information, to ask him why. But he held off, and the desire passed. The reason didn't matter. He imagined bashing George's head in with a studded club.

This thought aroused Julian.

Directly in front of Julian sat Bradley Smith, the cliché high school jock—tall and strong, stylishly quiff hairstyle, a charming smile few girls could resist, and the skull innards of a slug. He dated Billie Standifer for a time, then Madison Farley, and now Bianca Hendrix, if Julian was up to date on the gossip.

Bradley drank three milks every day at lunch. He had an 80s-era Chevy pickup with flashy rims waiting for him when he turned sixteen. He stayed after school every day to practice football, even when it wasn't required. He failed the state exams in the eighth grade, but was allowed to advance to high school anyway.

Bradley shit his pants at school in the third grade.

Julian was sitting next to him in class when it happened.

Even now, Julian remembered the smell.

He imagined shoving a sharp ice pick into Bradley's urethra, while shoving a powerful magnet into Bradley's ass. Would a powerful enough magnet pull the ice pick straight through?

This thought aroused Julian.

"What about you, Julian?" Mr. Scofield said. "What did you think of the ending?"

Julian sighed, looking at the wall above Mr. Scofield and above the blackboard. Then he said with complete seriousness, "Robert Jordan was a fool."

"Really?" Mr. Scofield said, chuckling under his breath, looking around the class for reactions that weren't forthcoming. "And why is that?"

Julian considered relaying a detailed answer but decided on a quick one instead: "He picked the losing team to play for."

Mr. Scofield laughed. "So you're suggesting he should have fought for the fascists?"

"Blindly fighting for any ideology or political movement is a fool's errand."

Mr. Scofield was talking again, trying to argue some senseless point, but Julian was done listening. His eyes moved over the students around him. Some of them looked back at him weirdly. Others appeared on the verge of slumber. He imagined them all dead. Some had their throats slit. Some were dismembered. Some had their skin peeled from their bodies. Blood everywhere. Bullet holes in each one. Bullet holes everywhere. Bullet holes and blood.

This thought aroused Julian.

He thought about the gun in his backpack, the Beretta 92FS, his dad's pistol.

Fourteen more minutes until he would be born again.

*

Julian understood Bradley Smith would have to be the first to go.

He didn't have anything against Bradley—he was a nice enough guy despite being the handsome jock type—but there were two factors guaranteeing he would be first to go: First, proximity; he was sitting directly in front of Julian, obstructing his view of much of the classroom. Second, his strength, athleticism, and overall courageous demeanor; if anyone in class was going to play hero when Julian started blowing heads off shoulders, it would be Bradley Smith.

Ol' turd in the trousers Bradley had grown up a lot since third grade.

Julian didn't particularly hate anyone; this wasn't about hate or revenge, and it sure as shit wasn't about being brainwashed by video games or violent movies. It was just something that needed doing. Sometimes, the world needed cleansing. Robert Jordan blew up a bridge for his cause. Julian Gibson was going to shoot up a classroom for his.

The cause was chaos.

School, rules, regimen—they were the opposite of chaos. The enemy of chaos. For however long Julian's attack lasted, he would have utter chaos all around him. If the responding officers were anything like the cowards in Uvalde, he would have a hefty chunk of time on his hands.

It wasn't about hate, but there was one particular boy who he would take immense pleasure in taking out: Kenneth Smartly. He was a snooty little prick if there ever was one, turning his lip up at anyone he saw as beneath him, pointing and laughing at the struggles or mistakes of others, spilling vile lies about every single soul when their backs were turned.

It was Kenneth who spread a rumor that still hadn't died down about Julian fucking his sister Mamie. Kenneth claimed to have caught them doing it behind the bleachers at the JV football game a few weeks back. This, of course, was ludicrous, seeing as neither Julian nor Mamie gave two shits about football, and neither of them did activities that required their attendance, like band or cheerleading. But once rumors got going, facts didn't matter a whole hell of a lot.

And now that Mamie was pregnant—Julian saw the positive test in their shared bathroom this very morning—the rumor mill would really get to swirling. The blabbermouths of Twin Oaks High would be ginning up stories of the oncoming birth of an inbred, mutant baby, courtesy of Julian giving his sis the ol' no clothes bump and grind.

It didn't matter Julian had never experienced sex.

It didn't matter that he didn't even enjoy masturbation.

Good, spicy rumors fly over all that bullshit.

But the rumors wouldn't matter a whole hell of a lot after today.

Suddenly, the classroom's intercom speaker crackled, interrupting Mr. Scofield's nonsensical lecture, issuing forth the short buzz meant to draw the attention of the students.

"Mr. Scofield," Principal Cruz said, her voice dull and crackling like an old radio, "send Julian Gibson to the office, please. Tell him to bring his things."

Julian glanced at the clock on the wall. He was supposed to get after it in five minutes. What now?

*

It wasn't as if he could pull steel with everyone staring at him.

That would ensure nothing went as planned.

"Fuck," Julian muttered, shoving his battered copy of *For Whom the Bell Tolls* into his backpack atop the Beretta. It called to him but he knew the time wasn't right. Bradley Smith or Mr. Scofield or someone else would pounce on him before he got two shots off if he pulled it out with all eyes on him.

"Watch the language there, Julian," Mr. Scofield said. "See you tomorrow. Happy Halloween."

Julian exited the classroom without another word, slinging his backpack over his right shoulder. His baggy jeans sagged as he made his way down the hall and he had to heft them up several times before getting to the office. The halls were oddly quiet, as they usually were when kids escaped the confines of the classroom with class still in session, and Julian's skater-style shoes squeaked on the glossy tiles as he walked. He passed by glass cases of trophies from sporting events of yesteryear and framed photographs of forgotten alumni and faculty.

Whistling an English shanty that his dad had played in the car this morning, Julian walked progressively slower, wondering what must have occurred that required his presence. Had someone died? Perhaps his grandmother—his mom's mom, living in a nursing home called the Dalmatian House—passed away. But he didn't think his folks would pull him out of class for that. Hell, they hadn't even paid her a visit in over a year. Who then? Mom or Dad? Had someone found out what happened to Uncle Archie, who disappeared a few years back while hunting with some buddies?

Julian had no clue, but kids didn't get yanked out of class unless someone died or they had an appointment of some sort. And he was certain he didn't have an appointment; not on a Tuesday, when Mom would be shaking her ass on camera so thirsty men would pour their savings into hers. (Mona and Jim weren't aware the kids knew about Mona's means of income, but they were; Julian had even watched several of her videos that had been pirated to PornHub.) So, somebody must have died. Julian found it a bit ironic that someone's death was preventing a whole host of deaths on this Halloween day.

Well, he thought, *not preventing; only delaying.*

He would get his chaos when the time was right.

Letting his whistling trail off, Julian swung into the open front office door. The desk lady pointed her thumb at the closed door of the principal's office.

"In there, Julian," she said. Her voice was somber in tone. Someone *had* died. He didn't wish death on either of his parents, but if it had to be one of them, he hoped it was his dad. He was nothing short of a complete mess, leading the family into financial ruin and swallowing pills with his whiskey every evening.

Julian tapped lightly on the door, then opened it slowly without waiting for a response. Principal Cruz sat behind her desk, bulging against her pantsuit in a most unflattering way. She bore one of those frowns that seemed to stretch to the bottom of her chin. Her eyes were glossy with spent tears. Sitting across from her was...

Who the fuck is this guy? Julian wondered, his face twisting in a confused manner.

He knew he recognized the man but couldn't immediately think from where. He'd seen him recently, of that he was certain. Julian stood there in the doorway, bag on shoulder, staring at the man, trying to remember, trying to connect the dots of why this man would be here apparently calling him out of class for some tragedy.

"Good morning, Julian" Principal Cruz said, offering a pathetic smile. "Sorry to pull you out of Mr. Scofield's English class."

"It's fine," Julian said, glancing briefly at the principal before looking again at the man, the wiry elderly man who...

"Did you happen to see your sister in the hallway?" Principal Cruz asked. "I contacted her Biology teacher but it seems Mamie went to the restroom a little while ago."

It was the old man from the haunted house, Julian suddenly realized, from The Dark Side of Hell, the guy who'd been sitting on the porch when they arrived there, ushering them inside beneath the glow of a kerosene lantern. He wasn't wearing the purple suit or top hat now—rather a brown-colored suit, complete with a vest, and his thin white hair was slicked back on his skull—but it was definitely him. In the light of the school fluorescents, he looked even more sickly than before. He was almost nauseously thin, like someone suffering from anorexia, his flesh more yellow than white—jaundice, Julian thought the word was. His eyes were dark yellow—orange even—at the corners, and as he smiled broadly at Julian, his teeth revealed themselves as the same shade.

But why the fuck was he here?

Julian didn't even know this geriatric fool's name.

"Julian?" Principal Cruz said.

"I haven't seen Mamie," he said, cutting his eyes to her. "Why did you call me here."

"Well," Principal Cruz said, pursing her lips, gesturing to the old man across from her, "your grandfather—"

"Julian, I'm afraid I have some bad news," the old man—who was most certainly not his fucking grandfather—said. "It's your parents."

Julian's eyebrows scrunched. What the hell was going on here? What happened to his parents and why was some haunted house loon bringing him information about them?

"Julian, they've been violently kidnapped and taken to The Dark Side of Hell."

"What?!" Principal Cruz cut in, her voice sounding like skidding car tires. "That's not what you said a min—
"

Before Julian had a chance to fully comprehend what was going on, the old man pulled a shiny revolver from inside his brown sport coat, his thumb working back the hammer, his forefinger pulling the trigger. Principal Cruz's brains splattered across the wall behind her as a loud *boom* filled the office.

Wide-eyed, Julian looked at the dead principal slumped in her chair, then at the wall beyond her, where her framed diploma was now marred with blood and bits. Looking back to the old man, Julian saw the revolver was now pointed at him. There were screams nearby, from the surrounding offices. An alarm bell sounded. Someone yelled that the phones weren't working and that the wifi had gone out.

"Time to find your sister, Julian," the old man said, his sick smile widening as he stood. He was incredibly tall; almost too tall for someone who looked so frail.

Julian wondered what time it was.

Was it 10:22am?

He was too confused and anxious to take out his phone and look.

One thing he knew, however: chaos had ensued.

NINE

The second gunshot convinced her that it was, in fact, gunshots she was hearing.

Mamie's heart was pounding so hard she could almost hear it, her breathing keeping pace, her eyes staring blankly at the tiled bathroom floor, her ears doing all the work. There was screaming. The alarm continued. From what she could ascertain from sound alone, the incident was taking place at the front of the school, near the offices.

She tucked the scalpel back into her jacket pocket and continued to listen, her hands shaking with fear.

Her school, Twin Oaks High, was the scene of a school shooting. It was something she only heard about on the news; never something she considered would actually happen at *her* school. Sure, Twin Oaks had its share of dirtbags but not anyone capable of opening fire on innocent teenagers. Right?

Apparently not.

She waited, still sitting in the stall. Staying where she was had to be the best course of action. The shooter or shooters would probably go for classrooms, to maximize death, not focus on bathrooms where, for all they knew, no one would be.

A series of for shots in a row.

Two more.

Three more in rapid succession.

More screams.

Running footsteps.

The constant buzzing of the alarm.

What Mamie knew now was this: whether there was more than one shooter or not, she couldn't be certain, but she was *absolutely* certain there was more than one gun. The sounds were different. Some shots had a loud *crack* sound, while others were more of a dull *bang* that seemed to shake the walls. Multiple guns could mean the cops had arrived and were firing back. But Mamie figured she would hear the shouts of cops if that were the case. Besides, it had only been a minute or two since the first gunshot. Surely not enough time for the PD or sheriff's department to bust in and open fire. So, more likely, there were multiple gunmen and they were having a field day.

Suddenly the door to the bathroom busted open, startling Mamie, causing her to shrink back against the toilet. She could hear a girl whimpering, sniffling, breathing loudly as if she'd just run a long distance.

Mamie inched forward, not wanting to make her presence known. She peered through the crack of the stall door. There, backing away from the restroom's door, shivering like a scared puppy was a blonde teenage girl. Seeing the girl's ponytail swing as she shuffled backward, Mamie thought she recognized her. Yes! She was a girl from Julian's grade, a freshman. She couldn't remember the girl's name at first but then there it was.

"Billie!" Mamie said, quietly but forcefully.

Billie Standifer gasped, turning toward the stall, her eyes as big as volleyballs.

"In here," Mamie said, cracking the stall door open a hair. "It's Mamie Gibson, Julian's sister."

Billie stood staring at her like she was frozen in time, as if nothing Mamie said was making sense. She was shivering and Mamie thought she saw a wet spot between Billie's legs.

"What the fuck is going on out there?" Mamie said, a little more forcefully.

"They're killing people," Billie said, her voice cracking.

"Who? How many?"

"What?" Billie said, suddenly looking about the restroom as if there may be gunmen waiting to burst from one of the stalls.

"How many shooters?!" Mamie was still whispering, technically, but demanding nonetheless.

"Wh—I don't know. Several, I guess. A few."

"Okay," Mamie said, thinking, "maybe we should stand on the toilet seats. That way if one of them comes in, they won't see our feet."

"Yeah," Billie said, but not really moving from her spot in the middle of the bathroom.

Mamie climbed atop the toilet in her stall, one of her black Doc Marten boots almost slipping into the bowl. She was about to encourage Billie to do the same when she heard shouting from outside the door:

"Mamie Gibson!" I loud, gruff voice said. "We're looking for Mamie Gibson! Once we have her, we'll leave! No one else gets hurt!"

Mamie gasped, her heart thundering even faster and

harder. She felt like she may pass out. What the fuck could anyone want with her, especially people shooting up a high school? She stood a little taller on the toilet seat, looking over the stall wall at Billie, still standing in the middle, her frightened eyes looking back at Mamie.

"Where is Mamie Gibson?" the voice yelled again, closer this time. "No one else gets hurt when we have Mamie Gibson!"

"Here!" Billie Standifer suddenly screamed out. "She's in here!" Her eyes dripped tears, still staring at Mamie. "I'm sorry," she said meekly.

Mamie trembled, fresh tears pouring down her own face. She may have been on the cusp of suicide just moments ago, but this wasn't what she wanted. She didn't want to be killed. She wanted it to be on her own terms. Perhaps she didn't even *want* to die. She might have pulled the scalpel back even if she hadn't heard the gunshots.

The bathroom door burst open, causing Billie to shriek in terror as Mamie ducked once more behind the stall.

"Where is she?!" a voice yelled.

"Th-th-there," Billie said, and Mamie could practically see her shaking hand pointing at her stall. Fucking bitch. "But p-please don't hurt her."

Fat chance of that, Mamie thought. She didn't know *why* these mysterious school shooters were after her, but it sure as shit wasn't so they could all sit down for a friendly game of D&D.

Then there was the deafeningly loud report of a gunshot, the bang instantly causing Mamie's ears to ring. She screamed out unintentionally, ducking down further, her hands going to her ears, her left boot slipping off the edge of the toilet seat, sending her toppling sideways to the tiles. Before she could right herself into at least a sitting position, the stall door was kicked furiously inward, banging off the stall wall.

Standing there where the stall door had been was a tall man in black coveralls, wearing a plastic jack-o'-lantern mask. He was holding an AR-15, and it was pointed directly at Mamie. Frozen with fear and on the verge of screaming or praying or pissing herself, Mamie saw beneath the stall walls to where Billie Standifer lay dead on the floor, the top half of her head missing, her blood and brains leaking out onto the shiny tiles.

"Let's go, bitch," the man said, reaching down with one gloved hand.

Without giving it much thought at all, Mamie brought the scalpel out of her jacket pocket, swinging it at the man's hand, catching his thumb, splitting the leather and flesh simultaneously. Blood sprayed from the wound and he yelped angrily and retracted his hand. But then the butt of his rifle was coming at Mamie, and there was no avoiding it.

Two masked men pulled Mamie from the restroom by her ankles, her bloody—possibly broken—nose leaving a trail of red as they went. Mamie was dazed and in pain, unable to follow the conversation of the two men. Nor could she make out the words of the older man they met in the hallway, though she could swear she recognized his voice.

And in the fog between consciousness and unconsciousness, she saw Julian standing not far away, looking at her with lively eyes. Whether that look was fear or excitement, she couldn't say.

TEN

Three black vans raced across Mangle County, each barreling toward a single destination.

In one of them, Jim Gibson was struggling to stay conscious. His head felt like it was in a vice. He was bleeding from several spots on his right arm and right thigh, as well as one small laceration on his cheek, all of which were caused by the glass of Sherry's window exploding inward. Weren't car windows supposed to be made in such a way that they didn't do that? Jim supposed when hit just right by a big fucking van, they would explode no matter what precautions went on during manufacturing.

Besides his head being rattled, Jim also had the Holy Trinity working its way through his system. Typically, the combination of Oxy, Soma, and Xanax just gave him a good, warm buzz, making his day enjoyable and worth it to keep breathing. He'd been using for long enough that he could function close enough to normal while swimming in opioid ecstasy. But when combined with a head injury, not so much.

There were three of them in the van with him, each decked out in black and wearing that ridiculous jack-o'-lantern mask. One was the old woman with the white hair, and she was driving; the other two were sitting in bucket seats in back, with Jim. One of them, morbidly obese, was holding an AR-15, which was pointed casually in Jim's direction. The other was holding what looked to be a turtle, of all things, its head and legs retracted into its shell.

"Wh-what are you doing with me?" Jim said, his eyes bleary and struggling to focus.

"You almost hit this here turtle, did you know that?" the pumpkin-faced person with the turtle said. Based on the voice and slender build, Jim realized it was a young woman. "It was crossing the intersection the same time as you. Guess neither one of you was paying close attention."

Jim looked down at the turtle, perplexed, the woman holding it forward as if he was supposed to genuflect before it. It was a decent-sized turtle for this area, maybe nine or ten inches in length and maybe six inches wide. What the hell was this woman doing? They didn't ram into his Mercedes because he was about to hit a turtle. He looked at her with wildly confused eyes, trying to peer into the dark eyeholes of the mask, though the dimness of the van prevented it.

"I heard a story about some kids south of here," the woman said, "that killed a turtle with fireworks. What do you think of that?"

"What?" Jim stammered "Why have you kidnapped me?"

Woozy as he was, Jim realized he could probably

take this masked woman head-to-head, seeing as she was unarmed except for a fucking turtle. They had not bound his hands and ankles like one normally assumed when contemplating the events of a kidnapping. But the man with the AR-15 was a problem. And he had no way of knowing if the driver was packing as well, though her geriatric ass could wield a hunting knife well enough to kill Sherry.

"Why did you kill Sherry?" he said, recognizing he had no clue if the knife used on his nurse had been left at the scene or if one of these goons had it sheathed on their belt or something.

"Answer the question, Doctor," the woman said, more firmly this time.

"What? Look, if Irish put y'all up to this, I can assure you we worked it all out. I just left there. It was just a misunderstanding."

"Focus, Dr. Gibson. The turtle,"—she held it up— "what's your opinion on a group of kids killing a turtle with fireworks?"

"What?" Jim stammered again. He shook his head, attempting to blink away his fogginess. What the hell did some story about kids killing a turtle have to do with anything? "It's awful. Killing a turtle would be awful." He shrugged, opening his hands up to display his utter incomprehension of the situation.

"So you're a turtle-lover," the woman said, nodding her head.

"Wha—not exactly. I have nothing against turtles, I suppose." Jim shrugged again, then asked, "Why did y'all take me, um, ma'am?"

"Ma'am," she said, looking over at the masked man beside her. "He called me ma'am. We have a real gentleman on our hands."

The man with the AR chuckled.

"Dr. Gibson," the woman said, looking back to Jim, "pull your cock out."

"What?" Jim said, the word seeming to be the only thing he was capable of saying, his voice going up an octave. "No, I'm not going to do—"

Before he could get the sentence out, the barrel of the AR-15 was at Jim's temple, pressing against him uncomfortably. He tried to scoot away on the floor of the van but the man inched forward, keeping it on him.

"Better do as she says, dipshit," the man wielding the rifle said.

"Yeah, Dr. Gibson, you turtle-loving prick," the woman said, "pull your cock out. Otherwise, Mukbang here will have to clean your brains off the floor when we reach our destination."

"But—"

"One more fucking word and you're gone, Doc," the man said, pressing the AR ever harder against his head.

Jim trembled, nodding slightly, a single tear clinging to the edge of his left eye. He was about to die. Norton Irish put a hit out on him and now he was going to die; but not before a healthy dose of humiliation. He thought about Mamie and Julian, about what they were likely doing at this moment, sitting in class for their typical daily routine, perhaps looking forward to watching some scary movies for Halloween. He thought about Mona, about what he *knew* she was doing, selling her flesh online so they could keep their nice four-bedroom, three-bath house, in the best neighborhood in Twin Oaks. And why? Because Jim Gibson had made—and continued to make—some extremely bad decisions. Now he was going to die for it. What would happen to his family now?

Jim worked his way from his bottom to his knees, his

whole body quacking with terror. His hands went to his belt buckle, fumbling with it clumsily as the tear fell down his cheek. He wanted to plead further, to beg for his life, to explain that he had a family, but the barrel pressed to his skull reminded him of the consequences of one more word.

Working free his belt, then unclasping the button of his slacks, Jim took hold of the zipper. He shuddered, not wanting to go any further. But the woman nodded slowly, and Jim could imagine the evil grin beneath her mask.

He unzipped and opened his fly, exposing the plaid boxers beneath, with its slit of an opening. Much like the turtle, Jim's cock had retracted as far away from the threat of danger as possible.

"Pull it out," the woman said. "Last time I'm telling you."

Grimacing, closing his eyes, Jim pulled down his boxers. Just a couple of hours ago his dick had been hard as a rock and sliding inside Sherry's snatch; now was a different story.

"You don't look very excited, Dr. Gibson," the woman said.

Jim shook his head, eyes still closed. For some ridiculous reason he felt as much embarrassed as fearful. This woman had stripped him of his manhood in mere minutes.

"Well, turtle-lover," the woman said, "let's see how much turtles love you."

Jim's eyes shot open and he looked down just in time to see the woman's gloved hands bringing the turtle forward, on level with Jim's shrinking cock. Jim gasped in horror, making a move to pull away. But then the man with the rifle spoke.

"Stay right the fuck where you're at!"

Jim shuddered, watching as his cock entered the opening of the turtle shell, right where the turtle's head would be, the shell itself now pressing against his pubis.

Nothing at first.

Jim thought perhaps they'd tricked him; it was an empty shell.

Then it bit, and Jim's cockhead exploded with pain, as if a scorpion had just sunk its stinger into his most tender of tender flesh.

ELEVEN

In a different black van, zooming down a farm-to-market road not far away from where Jim Gibson was, with his cock in the mouth of a turtle, was another cock aiming for another mouth.

Mona had yet to awaken from her crowbar-induced siesta. She lay on the floor of the van in her orange lingerie, her face caked in a sick combination of blood from where she was hit and the ultra-foul diaper shit that had been smeared across her face. Crumpled there in a weak fetal position, her mouth hung open in an O, with a brown stream of drool swaying with the movement of the van.

The smaller of the two captors in the back of the van had lowered himself to his knees and unzipped his black coveralls, pulling out an erect, veiny cock that Mona might have been impressed by in a more romantic situation. In her current situation, however, she was out cold, enduring a nightmarish dream of drowning in a giant, sweltering vat of shit, the sound of the van's engine morphing into the sound of the rolling boil of diarrhea in her mind.

"She gonna wake up and bite your peter off," the other man in the back of the van said in a high-pitched voice, the crowbar laying across his lap, an AR-15 leaned in the corner behind him.

The man hovering over Mona faltered, his cock losing a bit of its stiffness. Maybe she would chomp down on him with those shit-crusted teeth of hers. That wouldn't be too damn good at all. Pulling the Glock he'd used to kill Mona's neighbor from the holster at his hip, he placed the barrel between her legs, pressing it hard against her pussy.

"Wake up, you dumb cunt," he said, slapping her hard across the face with his other hand.

She was being lifted out of the boiling vat of shit, her head and body aching, her every sense taking in shit. She could taste it and smell it—both the worst taste and worst smell she'd ever experienced. Someone had been cooking her alive in the runny bowel movements of sickly nursing home patients. But now she'd been pulled free, just moments before her death. She could still feel the heat and dampness of it. But the heat was from the rush of adrenaline she'd experienced while trying to fight off the men, and the dampness was the sweat beading across her body. Mona's eyes, despite being caked together with some mutant baby's diaper surprise, opened groggily.

Then she felt it—there was something pressed between her legs, hard against her vagina. She jerked, meaning to get up and get away. But then she saw the jack-o'-lantern mask above her, shadowy eyes staring madness back at her.

"Listen here, you little whore," the man said, "you

chomp down on my johnson, I'll blow a hole so big in your cock-pocket, even the biggest dildos you can find would just drop right in. You got that?"

It was then Mona noticed the dick pointing at her, mere inches from her face. It was dark pink with the blood of arousal, and a glistening speck of pre-cum clung to the tip.

"Please don't," Mona muttered, tears forming in her eyes.

"Shut up," the man, cramming the pistol harder against her flesh. "Just suck!"

With that, the man inched forward on his knees, pressing his cockhead against Mona's dirty lips, the Glock pressing even harder against her vagina. With a whimper of disgust, her lips parted, the taste on her tongue still swimming with sourness and rot. The dick slid forward, not slowly or sensuously, but ramming into her mouth, greedy for whatever pleasure Mona's shit-caked maw could offer.

The man grabbed the back of her head, pulling her head to him as he thrust ever harder into her. Almost instantly, he was grunting with the ecstasy of good sex.

"Oh yeah, baby, baby, so good, that's it, fucking whore, oh yes, that's my little whore, my piggy, my little squealing piggy, yeah, choke on it, oooohhh, that's a good whore, my good little piggy…"

Mona's eyes squeezed tight together, tears streaming. She gagged on him with each thrust, the resulting saliva making the task ever sloppier. All the while, the taste and smell of that rancid baby shit permeated, seeming to grow harsher as her nares flared to breathe.

The man was on the brink of climax. Mona could feel his grip tighten on the back of her head, while the pistol on her privates grew lazy, softening. His thrusts became jerky as his body quivered with the initial pangs of orgasm, his grunts losing any sense of actual words.

She couldn't hold back anymore.

Not knowing what would happen, she certainly tried to hold it back.

With the man's grunts turning to wails of bliss, Mona vomited all over and around his cock.

"Goddammit!" he screamed, jumping back as hot bile spilled out across his lap, a combination of the oatmeal, blueberries, and coffee Mona ate for breakfast. Then he let out one brief yet violent yelp, and a single stringy strand of cum spit from his dick, falling in a sad arc to the floor of the van, so minuscule a load that it didn't even make a splat.

The man in the seat with the crowbar howled with laughter.

The driver yelled asking what happened.

"Goddammit!" the man before her yelled again.

Mona, vomit still hanging from her lip, peered up at him with worried eyes.

"You stupid cunt. You ruined it." He brought the Glock up from between her legs and whipped her across the face.

TWELVE

In the third van, only one pumpkin-faced man stayed in the back with Mamie and Julian. It should have been two.

After the two kids were thrown in the back, the old man in his brown suit took the driver seat, with one of the masked men taking the front passenger seat. The other one was seated in back with them, his bucket seat facing Mamie and Julian. He held one of those AR rifles in his lap.

Like her parents currently were, Mamie was dazed from a blow to the head. But she still had her wits about her. Julian appeared to be unharmed. Seated beside her cross-legged in the floor of the van, he stared blankly up at the masked man. If there was any apprehension to their situation, she couldn't detect it on her brother's face. He seemed content. Maybe even in awe of the circumstances.

"Why did you take us?" Mamie said, holding back tears.

The man said nothing. Didn't even move.

Julian, though, looked briefly over to her, as if noticing her presence for the first time. He looked, blinked, then looked back at the guy with the rifle.

"Are you going to hurt us?" Mamie said. Her stomach was a twisted ball of nervousness. Clearly this was a dumb question. Of course these psychopaths were going to hurt them. They already had hurt *her*, not to mention killed God only knew how many people at the school.

Quickly confirming Mamie's musings, the man nodded silently.

She sniffled, unable to hold it back. "Are you going to kill us?"

The man's right hand came off his rifle and formed a thumbs-up.

Then the tears fell, as if this confirmation was all she needed to open the floodgates. Regardless how close to death she already was when this madness began, she didn't *want* to die, certainly not by the hands of a gang of crazies. She'd wanted to die earlier, under her own terms. But now, as violent death stared her in the face, she wanted to defend life. Hers and, for what it was worth, the life of the thing growing inside her. She had to get away. Whatever happened when she escaped these nutbags, she'd worry about when the time came. She leaned over close to her brother.

"Julian, we've got to do something," she whispered. "We can't just let them kill us."

Julian blinked, his head turning slightly. He nodded but said nothing. That didn't seem like much help, but then what was Mamie expecting? Did she think Julian should take the lead in some sort of *Great Escape* scenario? Of course not. But she did need a reaction from him, and at least she got that. They would have to make a move sooner rather than later. The longer they were in the custody of these men, the closer they were to death. Both of their phones had been taken and smashed at the scene, so that wasn't an option. Maybe when they got where they were going, when the door of the van was slid open, they could make a run for it.

As Mamie considered their options, the sound of their travel changed. They had pulled onto a gravel road—she could hear and feel that gravelly crunch. Looking up toward the windshield, she saw a familiar cluster of trees. Then it hit her: the kidnapper driving, whom she was certain she recognized, he was the creepy old bastard from The Dark Side of Hell.

Their school had been shot up and they'd been taken by...haunted house performers?

Mamie turned to whisper this bit of information into Julian's ear.

But Julian was doing his own thing. He unslung his backpack, which the captors didn't bother taking for some reason, and unzipped it. Mamie chanced a glance at the guy in front of them. His head was tilted, as if he were watching them with curiosity. As if he were thinking, *What the fuck is this kid doing? He gonna chunk his Algebra book at me? It's not like this little prick has a gun.*

Yet, to Mamie's utter shock, that's exactly what Julian pulled from his backpack. It looked very much like their father's Beretta, something typically kept in his nightstand. The grip looked fat in Julian's rather small thirteen-year-old hands. Julian brought it up quickly, flicking the safety with his thumb, as if he'd gone over this scenario in his head.

Perhaps even more shocked than Mamie was the guy

sitting across from them. He yelped an unintelligible curse, fumbling with his rifle as he brought it up. But Julian had the pistol up first, and as he pulled the trigger, the man ducked, and the man riding in the passenger seat was in the direct line of fire. His head exploded across the inside of the windshield, the crack of gunfire so loud— even louder than in the restroom at school—that Mamie's ears were instantly ringing again.

She watched in petrified awe and horror, everything seeming to move in slow motion, as Julian pulled off another shot, this one hitting the guy's inner thigh in front of them, causing him to howl with pain.

The van swerved and the old man yelled.

Gravel kicked up around the van.

They were skidding to a stop, a cloud of dust billowing around them.

The old man turned around in his seat, screaming something.

The blood and brain matter on the windshield looked orange against the daylight outside.

Despite the wound to his thigh, the man brought the AR to his shoulder and aimed it directly at Julian.

The van was once more filled with the music of gunfire.

*

Without even pulling the trigger this time, the second guy's head burst open, his orange mask splitting and erupting outward in a flood of blood and brain matter, much of the mess spraying across Julian's face and shirt. The guy slumped forward, toppling to the floor of the van, right on top of Mamie's feet.

She was screaming, Julian realized. Screaming and

crying and being all hysterical, like he pretty much imagined girls would be in a shooting situation. But, hell, she'd kind of prompted this when she said they had to do something.

Only, Julian wasn't who shot the second guy in the head; he'd killed the first guy and hit the second in the leg, but he hadn't killed him. The fatal shot had been delivered by the driver, the old man from the haunted house. His silver revolver was pointed at Julian now, at the end of his thin, outstretched arm.

"Well, ain't you full of surprises?" the old man said, gritting his yellow teeth. "I couldn't have Necrosis knocking you off before it's time. Now, drop the fuckin' gun."

Julian's heart pounded in his ears.

He blinked away specks of blood in his eyes.

He shook his head, raising the gun toward the old man.

"Fine," the old man said, and the van was rocked with another loud boom, the flash of the revolver much more impressive than that of the Beretta.

More than thirty seconds passed before Julian realized he'd joined his sister in screaming. Another thirty seconds passed before he looked down at what was left of his hands. He'd been gripping the Beretta with both hands. The old man hit them both with one shot, somehow. Indeed, he'd blown off the forefinger and middle finger of both hands.

"No more pulling triggers or flipping people off for you, you little shit," the old man.

With that, the van started moving again. After just a minute or two, they passed the sign they'd seen the week prior. They'd returned to The Dark Side of Hell.

THIRTEEN

Jim Gibson's eyelids peeled apart with the stubbornness of two exhausted lovers.

He'd been on benders before. He'd been blackout drunk, so strung-out on coke he thought his heart would explode, and so high on heroin he'd been rushed to the ER and administered IV Narcan. He'd been through a lot of shit over a lot of years, but he'd never in that time experienced the horrid dreams that'd just passed through his head. And he'd never woken up to hallucinations of his family sitting around him, passed out and beat to shit.

The wild, horrifying nightmares were fading. All he remembered were screams and torture and blood. But the terror of them hung all around. Perhaps he was still in a dream. Yes, that made more sense than anything.

What did I take? he thought, trying to recall. But he wasn't even sure what day it was. His body ached, his head throbbed, and even his dick hurt. He hoped to hell he hadn't fucked some disease-infested hooker while on his latest bender. Pissing fire for the next month was all he fucking needed.

He looked around him. He and his family appeared to be sitting in a dining room—a grungy, dirty dining room, with smears of disgusting-looking substances on the walls. They were seated around a long, rectangular dining table, which was as old as Satan himself. It was warped and split in certain spots, but thick and probably sturdy. There were several chairs on each side and one at each end. Only four were occupied, and all four of the occupants were bound with chains around their arms and torsos, including Jim himself. Jim craned his neck, seeing that several feet behind his left shoulder was a single slender window, sporting a pair of ancient off-white drapes, riddled with holes. It appeared to be evening, maybe 6:30 or 7pm. Turning back, Jim looked to the ceiling, at the light there. It was not bright, with much of the luminescence not reaching the room's corners, but it glowed a spooky orange glow.

Then Jim realized where he was—or, at least, where he *thought* he was. Because surely this was a horrible dream that had been going on for some time. And in this part of the dream, he was in The Dark Side of Hell.

But then, as memories of the spook house came back to him, so did memories of what day it was and what events happened earlier, not long after he'd fucked Sherry and gotten intimidated by Norton Irish.

The wreck.

Sherry being murdered.

The captors with the jack-o'-lantern masks.

The turtle…biting his cock.

"Jesus fuck," Jim muttered.

Wriggling about in the chair, he quickly concluded that the chains were secured tight, likely locked in the back of the chair. He looked around at his family again, each of them in a state of post-battle slumber, probably brought on by both trauma and some kind of sedative. Julian was sitting a couple of seats down from him. Mona and Mamie were on the other side of the table, with his wife seated directly across from him.

Her head was hanging limp, but Jim could see that her face was dirty, as if someone had tried to drown her in mud. There was a huge knot at the center of her forehead, with a stream of dried blood lining each side of her nose down to her chin. Another bleeding wound was present on her right temple. Judging from the bra straps and the visible flesh of her shoulders and between the chains, Mona was in the Halloween-spirited bra and panties she'd recently purchased online.

What had she gotten into? Surely Norton Irish hadn't sent people to kill his whole family. That wasn't something Irish did. Was it? That would come off a bit excessive for not writing enough scripts for Oxycontin. Anyway, why the fuck were they in the shitty haunted house?

"Mona," he said, quiet but curt. He didn't want to be too loud because; surely, they were being watched by *someone*. "Mona, wake up."

With about the same speediness as Jim's own waking eyes, Mona's opened. She looked up at him with a glossy gaze, a string of drool hanging from her bottom lip. Jim wasn't sure she was even seeing him.

"Mona, do you know what's going on? How did you get here?"

She grunted, appeared on the verge of vomiting, then squeezed her eyes closed. Upon opening them again, she first looked sleepily down at her chains then around the room, her neck seeming to barely have enough strength to keep her head upright.

"Do you kno—"

"We're at that haunted house," Mona said groggily.

"Yeah," Jim said, relieved that her mind was at least somewhat there. "Who brought you here? Do you remember?"

She scrunched her nose, thinking for a moment. Then: "They killed Tilly." Her voice was sad yet somehow nonchalant, like she was talking about a character in a movie.

"What?" Jim said. "Tilly McGuire? The neighbor?"

Mona slowly nodded, her eyes blank, as if her mind was busy replaying whatever horrendous acts she'd been through.

"Fuck," Jim said. "Who was it? Do you know who did this and why and—"

"It's the old man," Mamie said from two seats to Mona's right.

Jim's head whipped to her. "Mamie...are you alright?"

"That's a bit of a silly question, Dad. Considering." Despite looking like she'd also been through Hell, with dry blood beneath her nose, her voice was remarkably even, her mind seeming far clearer than Mona's.

"Right," Jim conceded. "Old man? What old man?"

"'Tis I!" came a familiar voice, scratchy yet commanding.

Strolling in with his arms outstretched in a welcoming gesture was the creepy, old bastard who'd welcomed them to the haunted house a week ago. Now, he wore a black and orange striped suit, accented by a black top hat with a bright orange band. His smile was broad and yellow, his eyes looking both excited and cunning. He gave a little bow to Jim then Mona, removing his top hat and sweeping it beneath his frame in an old-fashioned manner.

"Let me welcome you to my home, The Dark Side of Hell," he said, standing upright again, looking between Jim, Mona, and Mamie. "And let me wish you a Happy Halloween!"

FOURTEEN

"And, furthermore, allow me to introduce myself," the old man said. "I am your host tonight, Colonel Gerald Granderson II. Let me say, we are all very pleased to have you here. Though, two of the family are, sadly, no longer with us—Necrosis and Trespass."

Colonel Granderson glared briefly over at Julian, whose eyes were still closed, his head hanging to the right, his pale face dotted with sweat and dry blood. If it weren't for the light rising and falling off his chest, Mamie would assume her brother to be dead. She couldn't remember much after Julian's hands were shot to pieces, except maybe someone injecting something into her arm, but she remembered blood being every-fuckin-where from her brother's hands.

"Now, I would like to introduce you to the rest of us. Everyone has dressed up so nicely for this special occasion. First though, we need to—"

"Why do you have us here?" Jim said, his nostrils

flared, clearly trying to assert some sort of dominance.

"Questions later, if you please," Colonel Granderson said, smiling snidely. "Now—"

"No! Fuck that! What do you want with us? We didn't do shit to you!" Jim wriggled in his chains, perhaps trying to loosen them. But if they were anywhere near as secure as the chains around Mamie, this was a fruitless endeavor, even being much stronger than she.

"I never said you *did* do shit to me, Dr. Gibson," Colonel Granderson said, looking a good deal more sinister now with his scowl at Mamie's father. "But as I just said, questions can be asked later. If you interrupt me again, I'll grab a pair of rusty pliers and pull out your tongue. And let me assure you, I *can* do it because I *have* done it before." He looked around at the rest of the family. "Not another word from anyone, unless you want things getting really nasty really quickly. Understood?"

Mamie nodded, as did her mother. Slowly, Jim followed suit.

"Great!" Colonel Granderson said, the smile returning to his face, exposing his yellow teeth. "Then we'll begin. But first, let's awaken the little shit."

Colonel Granderson took two long steps over to Julian's side of the table, then slapped him hard across the boy's left cheek, ushering from him an instant squeal of pain. Jim seethed, leaning as best he could in Julian's direction, the veins in his neck and head jutting out.

Even in this current horrifying predicament, Mamie found it borderline comical to see her father trying to play protector. He'd rarely, if ever, played that role in her sixteen years of life.

Colonel Granderson eyed Jim, waiting for a word or two to slip from his lips, as if he couldn't wait to snatch that tongue out of his mouth. Then he looked back at

Julian, whose eyes slowly opened.

"Sir Julian," he said, leaning down, only a few inches from his face, "I've just informed your family that if any of you say a word—one single word!—without me first giving you permission, I will yank your fucking tongue out of your head. Now, is that clear? Nod your head if you understand!"

Julian, wide-eyed now, nodded.

"Good!" Colonel Granderson said, standing and spinning around proudly. "Because I know *you*, Julian, understand how serious a man I am. Seeing as I shot your fucking fingers off."

Spinning back toward them, biting his bottom lip with anticipation, Colonel Granderson looked from Jim to Mona and back to Jim several times, each of them with shocked expressions, Mona with tears dribbled down her dirty face.

"Very good, very good, Gibson family!" he said. "I'd honestly expected one of you to say something with that revelation. Let me assure you, I bandaged Julian's precious little hands wonderfully. Many years ago, I was a surgeon in the army. So you may trust my expertise in these matters. And if Julian's poor dick-beaters become gangrenous, I have all the training necessary to amputate."

The smile never left his face.

"Now, on with the introductions. Each of you have met certain members of the family here, for they're the individuals who assisted in bringing you in. But allow me to introduce them to you formerly. Music please!" he yelled over his shoulder, clapping his hands as he said this last part.

Seconds later, an ensemble of creepy sounds issued from crackling speakers throughout the house. Hooting owls, thunder, ghostly winds, moans and screams of agony. Mamie was certain the track was no different than what one heard in haunted houses or costume stores everywhere this time of year. This was probably being streamed straight from some Halloween-themed channel on YouTube. Any moment now an ad for erectile dysfunction medication would pop on.

"First, let me welcome Playground!" Colonel Granderson exclaimed.

Mamie was facing her father and brother and the wall with the window, so she had to turn her neck to the left, looking past her mother to see who was entering the dining room from the entryway there, with the colonel excitedly waving his arm.

In strolled a man of average height and build, wearing a long tan trench coat like the types worn in detective movies. This man whom Colonel Granderson referred to as Playground was clean-shaven, with a weak chin, and had balding blond hair. He bore a subtle smile and greenish eyes that Mamie thought saw disdain in everyone they fell upon.

"Playground gets his name from his favorite stomping grounds," the colonel said. "He frequents all the playgrounds of Mangle County and beyond, from the small ones to large ones, always watching. Watching the little children, waiting for them to be alone." Colonel Granderson smiled in a way that suggested he was proud of this man. "Thank you for joining us on this Halloween night, Playground."

Playground smiled and nodded to Colonel Granderson, then quickly flung open his trench coat, exposing his pale, hairless body, nude except for bright orange briefs that bulged in the front, likely a thong in the back. Then he closed the coat back and walked around the other side of the table, passing Julian and Jim and sitting near the end, almost directly across from Mamie.

"Next, Mukbang!"

The floorboards creaked with his every step. Walking into the dining was an extremely overweight black man, wearing no clothes aside from an orange and black striped necktie around his fat, multilayered neck, the tie hanging only just past his sternum. He also wore a diaper, and Mamie shuttered to think what kinds of massive shits could fill that fucking thing. Mukbang's belly roll sagged over the front of his diaper. His neck, cheeks, and much of his torso were covered in zits, pinkish grey against his dark flesh. Some of them oozed purulent discharge.

"Mukbang gets his name from his daytime occupation. Much like you, Mrs. Gibson," Colonel Granderson smiled wide at Mona, "he has lots of followers of his videos." Thank you, Mukbang, for being here. Happy Halloween!"

Mukbang nodded, his chubby cheeks making way for a smile, then we walked past Mona, past Mamie, and sat directly beside her, the chair whining under his weight.

"Next—and, Dr. Gibson, I believe you got to meet her a little bit in the back of the van—is Lady Spermjacker!"

Mamie noticed Mona glance over at Jim even before this Lady Spermjacker entered the room. Mamie was aware that her father wasn't the most loyal husband on the planet—and, hell, his wife fucked herself on camera—but surely he hadn't screwed someone while also being kidnapped. But once Mamie witnessed her strolling seductively into the dining, she thought perhaps that wasn't too much of a stretch.

The woman, her hair long and dark and full, her eyes

as deep blue as the ocean floors, her lips full and red, was wearing black lace lingerie—bra, panties, garter, and stockings, all of it fitting her beautifully, as if she were a model from a magazine. She blew kisses at everyone as she made her way to Colonel Granderson, whom she then pecked on the cheek. While doing this, Mamie noticed a single orange bow in her hair. If ever there was a woman who could lure a man into sex in any situation, it was this woman.

"Lady Spermjacker gets her name from what she does best," the colonel said. "There's never been a man— or woman, for that matter—that she's failed to bust their nut. We're ever so happy to have you here, Lady. Happy Halloween!"

Lady Spermjacker, her hips swaying in mesmerizing fashion, walked around the table and sat between Julian and Jim, slapping them both on the thighs as she sat.

"And next we have Cuckoo!" Colonel Granderson yelled. "Mrs. Gibson, if I'm not mistaken you shared an intimate moment with him earlier today."

Now it was Jim who glanced over at Mona, their eyes meeting. If they happened to survive this ordeal, which Mamie thought was highly unlikely, there would no doubt be some closed-door discussions between the ol' parents.

Cuckoo was a shorter-than-average man, thin and scruffy, his beard growing in odd curly patches, his brown hair long and shaggy. He wore a three-piece black suit which appeared two sizes too large. He didn't smile or acknowledge the others, simply taking his steps, his hands in his pockets.

"Cuckoo gets his name because he's just plain crazy," Colonel Granderson said. "A real nut-job, Cuckoo has spent almost his entire life in mental institutions, ever since he killed his parents and his baby sister when he was five. Such promise at such an early age. Thank you, Cuckoo. And Happy Halloween!"

Cuckoo, still showing little to no reaction, took a seat next to Mona, who instantly looked away from him, as if in disgust.

"Last, but certainly not least," Colonel Granderson said, "I'm pleased to present Plastic Monster!"

Striding in, straight-backed and robotic, was a man of feminine appearance but gargantuan size, as if a medieval Viking tried to transform himself into an ultra-gay hipster. His reddish-blond hair was neatly styled. He was clean-shaven and his nose and lips were clearly products of plastic surgery; the lips especially, being as they were insanely full, comically so. And, if Mamie wasn't mistaken, the man's chin had been altered too, looking far too square and symmetrical to be real. He wore a perfectly measured suit of orange, with three different shades split between his jacket and pants, his vest, and his tie.

"Plastic Monster gets his name from his obsessions: cosmetic surgery and monstrous acts of sexual violence." The colonel smiled and winked at Mamie's mother. "His cosmetic enhancements are not restricted to the facial area, Mrs. Gibson. He's quite the specimen. Thank you for being here on this wonderful evening, Plastic Monster. Happy Halloween!"

As Plastic Monster walked around the table, Mamie looked below the man's waist, noticing the shifting position of a giant phallus beneath his pants with each step. It was like a thick pendulum swinging from one thigh to the other. Mamie wondered how much that sucker must have cost. And she hoped to hell it wouldn't be used on *her* tonight.

"Thank you, thank you, everyone, for being here,"

Colonel Granderson said, his arms outstretched again as he moved to the chair at the head of the table, standing behind it. "The Gibson family, meet my family—the family of Jack from The Dark Side of Hell. Family, meet the Gibsons, the typical American family."

He gestured to Jim. "We have the derelict, drug addict father."

He nodded to Mona. "We have the whore mother."

He winked at Mamie. "We have the knocked-up teenage daughter."

Mona looked over at Mamie, her eyes wide with surprise. Mamie avoided eye contact.

Colonel Granderson pointed to Julian. "And we have the school shooter son. Happy Halloween to each of you!"

FIFTEEN

Knocked-up daughter and school shooter son? What the fuck is he talking about?

Mona wanted to ask Mamie what the hell this old coot was jabbering about, wanted to spit in his face and tell him he's a goddamn liar. But she knew the threat about the pliers was genuine. Her splitting headache and the still-rank taste of shit and vomit in her mouth were all the convincing she needed. Not to mention the murder she'd witnessed of their neighbor. This old bastard—this Colonel Gerald Granderson II, or whoever the fuck he really was—might be a liar about some things, but not about the pliers, of that Mona was certain.

Mamie couldn't be pregnant, could she? Mona wasn't naïve enough to believe her daughter hadn't messed around with boys a time or two. Or maybe even girls; such things seemed in vogue, after all. But surely she had enough brains between her ears to use protection with a boy.

Julian on the other hand—the colonel's claim of him being a school shooter was ridiculous. He simply wasn't that type of boy. He was quiet, reserved. He enjoyed playing video games and watching TikTok and all the other stuff modern kids enjoyed. He wasn't the violent type. Mona didn't know why this school shooter claim hit her in the gut so hard. Certainly, it upset her because it was untrue (if her boy had been caught plotting some sort of attack at a local school, she was pretty damn sure she'd have heard of it), but also because the claim felt almost...*possible*. She didn't know why she thought this, and she hated herself for it.

None of this mattered at the moment, however. What mattered was that Mona and her family were chained to their chairs in a house full of crazy people. And if anyone thought the violence of their capture was over, they were dead fucking wrong on that account. They were brought to be active participants in some kind of sick Halloween party for psychopaths; rather, they were the party favors, the instruments of joy for the roisterers.

They had to find a way out of this.

The look on Jim's face told Mona he felt the same.

The concerned look of Mamie suggested she would bolt the second she was able.

Julian's pallor, stoic appearance, however—had his hands really been shot off? Mona wished she could lean beneath the table and have a look. Poor Julian looked as if he'd already given up, as if he'd accepted all of this.

"I do need to introduce two more individuals," Colonel Granderson said, looking pleasantly about the table at his guests. "We could not commence Halloween dinner without them." He turned to face the doorway, which Mona couldn't see out of past the first foot or so from her angle. "Please, Mother and Spawn, join us in the dining room."

She could hear the slow shuffle of pained footsteps, steps that weren't leaving the floor but dragging upon it with each motion forward. Mona remembered the last several months of her father's life, when his legs had swollen with fluids from congestive heart failure. She'd waited on him through those long days, as if what he'd done to her never happened as if the fun-filled fishing trips were all that mattered. Perhaps they were. Perhaps the good memories were always what mattered. During those last days, he could barely walk without becoming short of breath, his breathing sounding like the last few rattling sucks on a straw in an empty milkshake. But when he did walk, his feet dragged across the floorboards of his dilapidated home.

His steps sounded just like what Mona was hearing now—a sad, shuffling gate, raspy from dry feet along wood boards.

Then there they were in the doorway, Mother and Spawn.

It hadn't occurred to Mona when Colonel Granderson mentioned them but now it was obvious: these were the individuals the man, who she now knew as Playground, told her about before smothering her with the foulest dirty diaper in the history of dirty diapers. Standing before her was the old woman kidnapped from the nursing home...and her child.

"Would you believe Mother helped out mightily this morning?" Colonel Granderson said. "She killed a certain nurse in the passenger seat of Dr. Gibson's car. Mother has done a great many services for us, despite her age."

Mona's thoughts hiccupped for a second, and she stored this information away for later. If there ever was a later.

The old woman, this Mother, was completely naked. She was a wad of sagging flesh piled upon walking sticks. Atop her thin, varicose veins-riddled legs was a sizable midsection that drooped like melting ice cream. The large abdomen melted over her pubic region, completely obscuring her pussy area, thankfully. Her tits sagged almost as far, nearly to the bottom of her belly. They didn't sag like teardrops; Mother's tits, rather, stretched like the bulbous drops of not-quite-warm super glue, emerging from the glue gun and hanging there at ever longer lengths, growing fatter at the end but never seeming to disconnect from the place of origin. That was Mother's tits—sagging for eternity, nearly past her belly. Were someone to measure the length of her absurdly long nipples, they might just discover the tits to have won out at long last, taking the lead—by a slim margin, sure—in their race to reach the floor before the belly.

Veins and wrinkled skin were everywhere upon this lump of pale flesh. Moles and skin tags and sun spots and all the wear and tear of age. Her fingers were crooked with arthritis. Her toenails were yellow and clawed. Whatever muscle moved her elderly frame, it was completely hidden beneath the horror of ages worth of lymphatic tissue. Mona could almost imagine this woman's skeleton being a completely separate entity from the meat which hung around it like a cloak of disease.

Her face was no better, creased like the sun-split ground of West Texas, seeming to melt and liquify before Mona's eyes, like cold syrup on warm pancakes. Her eyes were sad in the truest sense of the word. Her mouth looked as if it hadn't held a smile in thirty years, the grimace which replaced it blending smoothly in with the creases down either side of her chin. Her hair was fluffy and wild, likely unkempt since the day she was taken.

Mother was an awful sight. But she didn't hold a candle to Spawn, whom she cradled in her sagging arms like a deformed possum she'd saved off the side of the road.

Whether Spawn was male or female, Mona didn't have the faintest clue. In fact, she wasn't even sure it was human; or wholly human. If ever there was a creature devised in a lab and sprouted from a test tube, it had to be this fucking abomination.

Its flesh was dark orangish yellow, like someone with severe jaundice but worse. The head was lumpy, as if it had been battered over the skull a few dozen times, and long strands of light red hair sprouted wildly in all directions, so fine that the outcrop looked like a smudge of orange just hovering there above that mutated skull. Its eyes were abnormally large and bulging from their sockets as if there was great pressure from the inside trying to force them out. Its ears, by contrast, were abnormally small, and the left one was pointed both at the top and the bottom, like a small fleshy wing. Its nose, too, was small, puglike, with both nostrils dripping with yellow snot. And its mouth was completely without lips, instead the flesh of its face growing directly into its gums, where the first few white teeth were just beginning to show, already growing at odd angles. Perhaps the worst part about this thing's face—*No*, Mona thought, *definitely the worst part*—was the absence of cheeks. Just as there were no lips, there were no cheeks. Below the cheekbone—the zygomatic bone, Jim could have told her—the flesh grew directly to the attaching bones of the skull, the maxilla and mandible, and from there into the gums; but where everyone else had that flap of skin on either side of their face, preventing entry from dust and bugs and any-fucking-thing, there was nothing but the open passage of air between the gums. Drool dripped from all sides in bubbly strands.

Much of the thing's body was veiled by Mother's clutching arms, but it appeared no better. Its arms appeared either naturally wing-like in their bent or contracted from nonuse. Its torso drooped in a similar fashion to Mother; though the orange flesh was smooth enough, there appeared to be too much of it, like the extra abdominal flesh of a person one-year post-op from gastric bypass surgery. Something grew from the left side of the thing's torso—the side more viewable by Mona—and it looked like an appendage of sorts or a very large skin tag, like a gnarled tree branch of flesh, sticking out three or four inches, with three other meat sticks growing off from it, no longer or bigger than toothpicks. Blessedly, the thing was wearing a diaper (Mona knew damn well what it did with those), and while Mother's forearm covered one of its legs, the one dangling down was thin and shiny with taut skin, hanging there limply, perhaps completely useless.

Jesus Christ, Mona mouthed silently.

"Mother," Colonel Granderson said, smiling pleasantly at her, "You have served us well the last year. Though you weren't chosen, like the Gibsons here or like the Marshall family before them, you have been ever so valuable to *our* family. We all thank you. And so does Jack, I assure you."

Mother said nothing. She stood there as if in a trance, her eyes glazed and staring into oblivion. A single strand of drool dripped from her mouth, landing between Spawn's eyes. It blinked, slowly, and uttered some throaty sound, likely the only sound it was capable of making without use of lips and cheeks.

But Mona wasn't thinking about this, at least not

consciously; she was thinking about the Marshall family. She remembered hearing about their disappearance on the radio last Halloween. They'd been residents of Stagsville, a twenty-minute drive from Twin Oaks. Their house—a nice, large country ranch—had burned to the ground Halloween morning. The burned bodies of three family dogs and two cats were found. None of the Marshalls ever were. To this day.

"And what an interesting surprise when you spit Spawn out of your fuck hole," Colonel Granderson said. "A surprise indeed. But that didn't slow down your nightly usefulness, did it?" The colonel laughed and looked around the table at his family."

"Not a bit," Mukbang said with a voice as deep as rhythm and blues itself.

"Fuckin' right," Cuckoo said, smiling devilishly.

"We had good times," Lady Spermjacker said, biting her bottom lip and looking disturbingly seductive with her gaze at Mother.

Others agreed and nodded.

"You're all absolutely correct," Colonel Granderson said. "But tonight, Mother, we must bid farewell. For all good things must come to an end, I'm afraid."

Still no reaction from Mother. Just that dumb, absent stare. Her sagging flesh was the only hint of emotion, and that emotion was defeat and the deepest, darkest sadness.

"Put Spawn on the floor, Mother," the colonel said, "then get on the table."

SIXTEEN

Mother dropped the deformed monstrosity known as Spawn. She didn't set it down gently and give it a little nudge to move it along; she just opened her arms and let whatever the hell Spawn was fall to the floor. Julian heard its head knock painfully loud against the wood floor.

"Oop!" the colonel exclaimed then laughed heartily, a laugh echoed by the rest of his family.

Julian was just glad to have that monster out of sight. Now that it was on the floor crawling or slithering about, the dining table blocked his view of the damn thing. The granny they called Mother was bad enough without that obscenity being in her arms. If Julian had his dad's Beretta right now, with only one bullet to fire, he'd put Spawn out of its fucking misery.

If he had an index finger to pull the trigger, that is.

Julian kept forgetting that. Half of his hands were gone. It stung down there, but the pain was surprisingly scant unless he shifted around a bit, in which case they

98

burned like a bad sunburn. They didn't hurt like he thought they should, though. He almost wanted them to hurt more, to hammer home the reality of what happened. As it was, with his arms pinned down beneath chains, he wasn't even able to *look* at his hands, much less feel the agony. His mind, still half delirious from whatever drug they'd dosed him with to knock him out, was constantly trying to convince him his hands were still there, intact as ever. It was all the work of his overactive imagination.

The dining table creaked as Colonel Granderson pulled the chair away from the end and Mother placed her hands on the table's lip and leaned with her considerable weight. Her mouth hanging open, grunting wordlessly, the naked old hag tried to pull herself up onto the dining table. Her left knee came up, just cresting the surface, and Julian saw a white scar across Mother's flesh there, likely the blemish of some forgotten knee surgery. If Mother had been here the last year or so, being raped repeatedly by this disturbed gaggle of nutcases, which was what Julian gathered from what the colonel and others were saying, then probably everything before her capture was forgotten. Whatever life she lived before arriving at The Dark Side of Hell was a memory so fleeting and meaningless that, for all intents and purposes, it never happened.

Which begged the question: was this what Julian and his family had to look forward to?

Mother was not having any success propelling herself to the tabletop.

Behind her, Colonel Granderson had leaned against the wall, crossing his arms and laughing as he watched the spectacle of this geriatric bag of bones try to climb a few feet off the ground.

To Julian's left, Lady Spermjacker snickered. She

slapped Julian's thigh for a second time as she watched Mother struggle. Her hand slid up Julian's leg, nearly to his crotch, and she squeezed, poking her sharp nails into the fabric of his jeans.

Julian shuddered, feeling hot. Even with the horror of this moment and the pain in his hands, he could feel his dick growing hard. He wasn't someone who thought much about sex. He rarely looked at porn and got most of his masturbatory material from watching videos of riots and terrorist attacks; though, he rarely masturbated either. He didn't like the release, the feeling of excitement whisked away by a spurt of cum. If he held it, his lust for chaos endlessly intensified.

But...as Lady Spermjacker caressed his inner thigh, Julian felt a lust for the opposite sex that had been mostly foreign until now. He wanted her hand to slide up further, to grab hold of his dick, to pull it out of his jeans and wrap her lips around it. He wanted to shoot his load into her mouth and—

"For fuck's sake," Colonel Granderson said, "someone help this fat bitch get on the table. Plastic Monster, do you mind? You know how my back gets."

"Not at all, Colonel," the large human next to Julian said, his voice surprisingly high and feminine. He stood, straightening his prim orange suit, and positioned himself behind Mother.

Mother's left leg fell back to the floor, the knee barely ever reaching the table's surface. She huffed exhaustion but her eyes appeared vacant, staring off at the other end of the table, where no one sat. Her jowls quivered though, whether from the strain of trying to get up or from some emotional distress.

Julian was curious which it was. He wondered, as Lady Spermjacker's hand slid sadly off his leg, what all the old woman had been through. In a way, he wished he could have seen it. Or, at the very least, to have all her torturous nights streamed to his phone so he could have a look over his after school PB&J.

Hiking his orange slacks, Plastic Monster squatted down behind Mother, wrapping his arms around her flabby thighs, his oddly smooth face resting against Mother's skin tag-riddled backside. He hefted her up and tossed her forward with relative ease, sending her flying probably a little higher than he meant. Mother landed smack-dab in the center of the dining table, her flesh slapping hard against the wood, her face and nose hitting hardest, making a single audible rap, like one solid knock on a door. She squawked something painfully, her face coming off the table twisted into an ugly grimace, her drooling mouth open wide, revealing not only her lack of teeth...but lack of a tongue.

Apparently Colonel Granderson—or someone, at least—did in fact have experience with tongue removal.

It was at this point, Julian noticed the smell. A sourness, putrid like rotten onions and must. It was strong now, and Julian's eyes went from Mother's face to her dimpled, flabby ass, her crack seeming to stretch on for miles. From his vantage, he couldn't see below the back of her thighs, where the crease of her ass crack became the crease of her cunt, but he was certain that was where the awful smell was coming from.

Julian's stomach churned. The smell alone was bad, but realizing where that odor originated from made it ten times worse. What the hell could be going on downstairs for this hag's twat to smell like Hell's landfill? She had to have some kind of disease, Julian figured, a disease where she rotted from the inside out, starting with her goddamn pussy.

For the moment anyway, the boner brought on by Lady Spermjacker had completely dissipated.

"Now then," Colonel said, clearing his throat as Plastic Monster once again seated himself to Julian's right, "Mother, roll over would you please?"

As Mother began the arduous process of moving from her belly to her back, Colonel Granderson stepped out of the dining room, disappearing around the corner. What the hell was going on here? Why was this Mother lady with the stinky hoo-ha lying atop the table like a holiday pig at a Hawaiian luau? Never mind the more important question—why the fuck were Julian and his family here to begin with?

"Pardon my manners for not setting the table ahead of time," Colonel Granderson said, returning with a stack of porcelain plates. Laid across the top of them was a large soup spoon and a serrated carving knife.

Mother had worked her way to her side, grunting in her weird tongueless way. Julian was none too pleased to note she'd decided to roll *away* from his side of the table, thus presenting her ass end in his direction. Though her saggy, lumpy backend wasn't directly in front of his face, it was fucking close enough. She broke wind—a quick, high-pitched fart—as she strained to get to her back. The smell, if there was one, did not overtake the scent of her sour mash.

Alas, Mother worked herself into a supine position, panting, staring straight up at the ceiling with those same dead eyes.

"Great!" the colonel said, setting the spoon and knife on the table. Then he walked about the table, setting an off-white plate in front of each attendee.

Julian was getting a really bad feeling about this. He looked at Mamie, whose eyes were wide with terror. Then to his mom, who looked green with disgust beneath whatever was smeared all over her face. Then he looked left, past Lady Spermjacker, at Jim, who looked to be frantically nodding his head toward the colonel, attempting to get his attention.

Colonel Granderson noticed: "Dr. Gibson, do you have a question?" he said as he reached the end, his seat, placing the final plate there.

Jim nodded vigorously.

"Okay then. Go ahead, Doctor."

"Please, just let us go!" Jim blurted out in a panicked voice. "We won't tell a fucking soul; I can guarantee it!"

"Dr. Gibson," the colonel said calmly, "I said you could ask a question. I did not say you could make ridiculous pleas to be set free." He leveled his eyes at Jim, his stare going serious. "Ask a question."

Jim, sweat dripping from his hair, looked at Mona, as if to extract a question from her mind, then looked back to the colonel. "Why are you doing this?! What is all this about?! Will you please let us go?!"

"Oh relax, Doctor," he said, waving a hand at Jim, smiling wryly. "It's just dinnertime. The real fun will come afterward. Now, Mother, spread your legs!"

SEVENTEEN

"Hey, wait—"

"No," Colonel Granderson said sternly, holding up a hand at Jim. "No more questions, Doctor."

Jim was about to protest further—he *had* to do something until he figured a way out of this nightmare—but then something brushed against his leg, causing him to yelp and flinch against the chains. It wasn't the whore, Lady Spermjacker (a fucking ludicrous nickname if there ever was one), not her this time.

Looking down, Jim saw it was the baby, the insult to nature—Spawn. It was seated at his feet, tugging now at his slacks with one contracted hand, one of its bulging eyes looking up at him, the other looking lazily at nothing. Snot dripped from its pug nose, plopping on the floor. Though his hands were chained tightly to his sides, Jim flicked his fingers at Spawn in a *Get the fuck out of here!* motion.

Instead, Spawn opened its gaping, cheekless mouth

and began gnawing on Jim's right leg, the copious amounts of slobber quickly soaking through his gray slacks, turning them dark. The thing's teeth weren't fully developed, not enough to sink into meat, so it was effectively gumming Jim's leg, the way babies gum everything within reach.

You look like a creature that was kicked out of a fantasy novel, Jim thought.

Then he kicked it off his leg, sending Spawn flailing beneath the table, cracking its noggin once more on the floor, this time at Mona's feet. She must have felt the thing fall before her, because Mona looked past the geriatric waste lying on the table, meeting Jim's eyes and scrunching her brow, as if to ask what the hell he was doing. Jim, however, in kicking the baby away, moved his chair slightly backward. He realized now his dining chair had wheels of some sort on the bottom. Whether he could use this new bit of information, he wasn't sure.

"Looks lovely," Colonel Granderson said, standing at the end of the table, staring between Mother's legs the way Jim would stare at a baggy of top-shelf heroin, a stack of gold coins, and a slice of twenty-year-old pussy. But, based largely on the smell, Jim guessed that wasn't what was between Mother's legs. "For Halloween," the colonel continued, "we added everyone's favorite treat." He paused, looking around the table with that always creepy, yellow smile. "Candy corn!"

What the fuck was this kook talking about? He had this old, flabby chick splayed out on the table like a prime piece of meat and he's talking about candy corn?

"Who's ready to eat?" the colonel said, snatching the carving knife off the table.

Mukbang's hand shot up with lightning quickness, a broad grin emerging between his chubby cheeks. He, Jim imagined, could loan Spawn some cheek meat and have plenty left over.

"Me!" Playground said.

"Always," Plastic Monster said.

"You better believe it," Lady Spermjacker said, slapping Jim and Julian on their thighs again, this time pretty damn hard. Jim felt her palm drive a piece of glass from his broken car window deeper into his flesh. That wreck seemed like many moons ago. He felt like he was in a different world now.

All of Colonel Granderson's goons appeared elated.

His heart quickening, Jim looked at the old woman, her saggy tits drooping to either side of her living carcass. He looked to Mona's worried eyes, to Mamie's pale face. He looked to his right at Lady Spermjacker biting her bottom, lip, at her full, perky tits, then to Julian, who looked on with what could be mild interest but clearly breathing through his mouth in an attempt to avoid the smell.

"Good!" Colonel Granderson exclaimed, and he leaned forward, dipping toward Mother's pelvis, the knife raised.

What the fuck was he going to cut?

Mother's legs opened further, as if she were waiting anxiously for this, and Jim could see better now. With arthritic hands, she pulled her sagging belly up, exposing a tuft of white hair. Jim couldn't help himself, he tilted his head to the right to get a better view, to see just part of the cluster of meaty folds that made up her worn-out cunt, like an old beat-to-death catcher's mitt wrapped in several layers of thinly-sliced roast beef.

Colonel Granderson's knife came down to the spot where Mother's inner left thigh met her pelvis, the sensitive spot where Jim would often kiss Mona (on the rare occasion they had sex) to send shivers through her body. The serrated knife sawed into her, quickly splitting her thin flesh. He sawed quickly, putting his weight into it. The blade was at least a foot long, and every time the colonel sawed forward on the lower pelvis, the tip of the knife cut into Mother's large, fleshy abdomen. Blood spilled from the wounds. It pooled, Jim saw, beneath her ass on the table, blood and...a yellowish-white substance.

Is that puss? he thought with horror.

Jim looked at Mother's face, her mouth agape, her nostrils flared, her eyes still staring blankly up at the ceiling. No screams of pain, no grimace, not an ounce of fight. A single tear zig-zagged along the wrinkles of her face, dripping into her ear.

"Why are you doing this?!" Mamie suddenly screeched, tears pouring down her own face.

The colonel kept sawing, laughing and sticking his tongue out at Mamie. Jim heard the rough grinding of the blade cutting through bone—Mother's pelvis.

"Osteoporosis!" he said, looking directly at Jim now. "It makes sawing through bone so much easier, wouldn't you say, Doctor?"

"Why *are* you doing this?" Jim said, repeating his daughter's sentiment, trying not to sound panicked. "You're going to kill her."

"Mother is well aware of her fate, Dr. Gibson. She knows the score. And do you see her fighting it? No. Now shut the fuck up before I saw off one of your kids' heads instead."

The red and off-white mixture of blood and what had to be puss reached the edge of the table and began dripping to the floor. Spawn shuffled beneath the table, and Jim looked just in time to see it positioning itself beneath drops of bloody puss, catching them in its monstrous open maw. Spawn was propped on its elbow, its arms too contracted to use its hands, and its legs were splayed behind it, one of them, Jim saw, appearing to be almost jelly-like, as if it were free of bones altogether.

He heard a crunch, and Jim looked back at Mother's lower half to see the knife had all but disappeared from view. Colonel Granderson was still sawing, the knife going through meat easily now, likely cutting into her colon and lower intestine, then into the fatty flesh of her buttocks. Then the blade knocked against wood, and the sawing stopped.

"One side done," the colonel said, straightening himself and twisting his back. He held the knife up, displaying its blood and shit-covered blade. Then he reached down with his other hand and plucked something from between her legs. Bringing it back up, Jim saw that it was a candy corn, caked in that off-white substance. "I get the first bite," he said, then tossed it into his open mouth.

"Please stop!" Mona suddenly sobbed.

"Yes," Jim said, staring frantically at the colonel. "Please, just let us go!"

"You know, Dr. Gibson," Colonel Granderson said, after swallowing the candy corn, "I think Playground may have told your wife about the severe bacterial infection *and* yeast infection Mother had when we brought her into our home. Nice and sloppy cunt with all that biological chaos going on down there. But, just for this occasion, just for Halloween, for the last month, we've made sure she kept all of our ejaculate locked up in her pussy too. Every night, one or two or three of us would fuck her, then I'd quickly stich her pussy up before our jizz spilled out on the bedsheets. The next night, I'd take the stitches out and we'd have our way with her again, sloppier than ever. I tell you, Doctor, that cunt of hers just kept getting better and messier with every day that passed. Can you smell the funk of it?" He waved his hands toward his nose pleasantly. "I filled her cunt with candy corn this morning, just to be festive."

"This is fucking sick, man!" Jim screamed, his pulse throbbing at his temples. "Just let us go! We don't want any part of this!"

"Awe," the colonel said, pooching out his lip, "you act as if you have a choice. You received the tickets, remember, Doctor? You were chosen."

"What? No! You gave us those tickets. You can pick someone else!"

"You misunderstand, Dr. Gibson—I didn't choose you; Jack did. And when Jack makes a selection, it's set in stone. Now, I'll not warn you again about speaking without permission."

Jim panted, feeling out of breath, as if he'd just run a couple of miles. Sweat dripped into his eyes, burning. Mona and Mamie were both crying. Julian, tough as he was, looked worried himself, like the realization of how horrible their situation was, was finally dawning upon him.

"Let me finish up here," Colonel Granderson said.

And so he did. The colonel sawed into the left side of Mother's pussy in the same fashion as the right, cutting all the way through and about a foot deep into her abdomen, no doubt slicing into intestines and colon and ovaries and probably even as high as the stomach. Blood and puss and rotten cum spilled out of her, covering much of the table in Mother's slop. At some point during this process, her eyes went from looking dead to really *being* dead. She never screamed or flinched or tried to get away. Not once.

Then Colonel Granderson cut crossways, at the top of her abdomen, connecting the two previous cuts. He sawed downward, just below the ribs, pulling back on the knife only when it hit the table. It took him several grueling moments to saw through Mother's spine, but he did it. It was a good knife, Jim saw.

When he was done cutting, Colonel Granderson stood back, panting. He removed his top hat and wiped his brow with his sleeve. After a deep breath, he spoke:

"Cuckoo, Playground, pull her from the table, would you?"

Without a word, Cuckoo and Playground got up from their seats and went to the opposite end of the table as the colonel. They grabbed Mother's corpse at the pits and pulled her from the table, dropping her in the floor without a care. The act left a streak of her blood-puss-cum-candy corn mixture across the tabletop.

And there, right in front of Jim Gibson, was what could only be described as a large lasagna-like loaf of meat and organs, consisting of most of her abdominal cavity *and* all of her reproductive system. A Mother loaf, for lack of a better term.

EIGHTEEN

Mona was sixteen again—lying in bed, dozing off with *Saturday Night Live* on her television and the latest issue of *Cosmopolitan* spread across her lap—when her father came into her bedroom, the walls decorated with the posters of her favorite pop stars, creeping up to the bed without a sound, then sliding into the sheets beside her, his breath smelling of cheap beer and cigarettes, as it always did on the weekends. No amount of *'Daddy, please stop'* made him stop. No amount of crying did either. He only stopped when his load was spent, and then he slinked out of bed without a word, his shoulders and head sagging. Mona thought perhaps he was ashamed of his actions, but he wasn't as ashamed as she. And she'd done nothing to deserve that shame.

That was the most frightened Mona had ever been until this day.

Now it seemed things couldn't get much worse. She'd been beaten, had shit rubbed in her face, been raped in her mouth, chained to a chair, and made to watch this most horrifying act—an elderly woman killed before her eyes in the most depraved way imaginable. Yet, Mona felt—no, she *knew*—things were going to get worse, if not *much* worse.

Before her, almost directly between Mona and Jim on the table, was a rectangular chunk of woman meat, complete with a tuft of white pussy hair at one end. And, Lord help her, Mona knew exactly what was coming next. There had been no hiding the fact that they were sitting down for dinner.

A round of excited chatter had arisen from the colonel's so-called family. Mukbang was starving. Playground said he loved the scent in the air. Cuckoo licked his lips repeatedly. Plastic Monster was laughing, his fat fake lips spreading in a rubbery way that Mona could almost hear. Lady Spermjacker was moaning to herself, her right hand cupping her right breast, squeezing, while her left hand was unseen to Mona beneath the table; the direction of her arm, however, suggested it was between her legs, likely rubbing or fingering.

"You sick bitch," Mona muttered, hating this disgusting woman more than she hated any of the rest. That such psychotic depravity could exist in someone so outwardly flawless and beautiful was revolting, beyond comprehension. What spurred even greater hatred was the fact that men would still blindly fuck this woman, no matter how sick and twisted she was. *Probably even Jim,* she thought. Then: *No, not probably; Jim would definitely fuck her, even after watching her eat a whole goddamn slab of geriatric dead chick.*

Mona glared at Jim but saw that his eyes were once more on Colonel Granderson, worried as ever.

"First, a little sauce," the colonel said, with that ever-present, ever-evil smile.

Mona's eyes went back to Colonel Granderson, seeing him lean down with the large soup spoon in hand. He pushed it, with very little effort, into the old woman's sloppy cunt. The knife, so far as Mona could tell, had not cut into Mother's pussy, rather cutting up the sides and then across her abdomen. So, presumably, while much of the sludge of rotten cum had spilled out during the carving process, there was still a good bit inside her honey hole.

This was confirmed as Colonel Granderson pulled the spoon back out, some of the putrid contents sloshing off the spoon's sides as he did. The spoon was full with thick, off-white rottenness, with streaks of yellow and pink and a dot of blood. Of course, there were several coated candy corn as well.

The colonel poured this first spoon of slop onto his own plate. Then in the pussy with the spoon again. Around the table he went, dishing out a healthy helping of cunt rot on each plate.

He dished out Julian's helping, and he appeared green as he gazed down at his plate. He'd always been a difficult eater. Broccoli, spinach, squash—no fucking way he was eating that shit without it being forced into his mouth by Mona or Jim. In his younger years, anyway. As he'd gotten older, they'd all but given up trying to make him eat veggies. Now he had a rancid puddle of cum and other infected bodily substances in front of him.

As the colonel dug deeper into Mother's smelly twat, the resulting contents appeared thicker and more...curdled. The scoop he splatted on Jim's plate was the consistency of cottage cheese, and the streaks of yellow so dark that it was almost brown.

By the time he got around to Mona, what he dipped onto her plate looked like a gooey rice crispy treat that had been heated in the microwave. It sagged on her dish in the semi-round form of the spoon. It was then Mona realized parts of the pussy platter were moving. There were maggots amongst the rot and candy corn. Because of course there were.

Mamie was given a helping of much the same consistency.

Then came the meat portions.

There were ten of them total at the table—the Gibsons, Colonel Granderson's five weirdos, and the colonel himself. Somewhere below the table was the mutant known as Spawn, and periodically Mona could hear him slurping something up. She thought she heard him at the other end of the table now, where the corpse of the old hag was. She shuttered to think what that little devil child was doing to her body.

Despite Mukbang's protests, Colonel Granderson gave everyone an equal portion of meat and organs. The colonel assured his obese minion that he could eat more later, that there would be plenty of leftovers. He sliced the meat into cube-like pieces, and when he spooned them onto plates, pieces of intestine and other organs spilled out the sides, as did the juices of shit and piss and cum and blood and Lord only knew what else.

It occurred to Mona, as her cube of Mother was placed atop her curds of Mother, that being chained to the chair, she had no means of eating. They would have to unchain the Gibsons in order for them to eat. But, whether they brought out their guns or knives or whatever, there would be no eating. Mona was going to fight and run and get the fuck out of this place. The second she and her family had their arms free, shit was going to go down. She wasn't dying in this place without a fight. And she sure as fuck wasn't eating that shit.

"Alright, now," Colonel Granderson said, back at the head of the table after divvying up all the Mother meat, "my dear family, please assist the Gibsons in eating while you eat yourself. As you can see, they have no means of putting the food in their mouths without help. Most importantly, everyone enjoy!"

NINETEEN

Mukbang's fat fingers grasped the layered chunk of meat, looking like a nightmarish cut of lasagna. Squeezing it gently, pinkish sludge gushed out around his thumb and liquidy shit oozed between his fingers. He wiped the meat through the cum-rot sauce, like a piece of garlic bread through marinara. Lifting it, the meat dripping, a piece of small intestine dangling, Mukbang looked greedily at it, licking his lips.

But this was not his piece.

Jim vomited from the other side of the table. Projectile-like.

Mona pleaded, trying to avoid her bite, but *in* it was stuffed. She hacked and gagged and vomited on the floor.

The colonel's family was laughing.

Laughing and eating.

Like they were eating freshly delivered pizza.

Julian, green and diaphoretic as he was, opened his mouth, his eyes as blank as Mother's had been, and accepted the bite into his mouth, delivered by Lady Spermjacker. He winced as he chewed. But he did not spit it out or vomit.

"Your turn, doll," Mukbang said with that insanely deep voice. He looked at Mamie almost pleasantly, as if he were a parent feeding his toddler child, feeding them a spoonful of veggies that they didn't want. "Your turn."

Tears rolled down Mamie's face.

Her bottom lip trembled.

She wanted this to be over.

She wished she'd sliced her wrist in the bathroom and been done with it.

Closing her eyes tight, balling her hands into fists, digging her nails into her palms, Mamie opened her mouth and accepted her dinner.

TWENTY

Jim Gibson thought he was going to pass out. He'd vomited so forcefully so many times, that he could swear blood vessels in his neck and temples had burst from the strain. His lap and the chains enwrapping his torso were caked in chunky puke. The sour smells of bile and the diseased, abused old woman hung in the air.

Light-headed, his chin to his chest, Jim was on the cusp of an uncomfortable slumber when the voice of Colonel Granderson slowly emerged, at first seeming far away and difficult to understand, like he was speaking from the bottom of a well. But then the voice was there like it had been, and Jim's eyes were fluttering open.

"—so we'll divide them up as best we can without our two deceased fellows," the colonel said, pausing briefly to look at Jim as he raised his exhausted head from his chest. "Welcome back, Dr. Gibson. Damn fine projectile vomiting on your part. I'd venture to say you've seen very few patients who could puke their guts up with that level of enthusiasm."

"Please, let us go," Jim said wearily.

"I'm afraid that's not possible," Colonel Granderson said.

"Why not?!" Mona screamed, her dirty face wet with tears. She too was covered in her vomit. It seemed Julian was the sole Gibson not to upchuck their Halloween feast.

"As I said, Jack chose you."

"Let me talk to Jack!" Jim said, his head becoming clearer. He had to get his family out of this fucking mess.

"Oh, trust me, you'll meet Jack when the time comes. But that time is not now."

"Take me to him!"

"Dr. Gibson, I still have those rusty pliers tucked away if I need to use them."

Jim gritted his teeth and flared his nostrils, but held his tongue to keep it from being yanked out.

"Lady," the colonel said, looking at Lady Spermjacker to Jim's right, "the good doctor is yours."

"Yay!" she exclaimed, clapping her hands excitedly. Then she grabbed Jim's vomited-covered thigh and whispered in his ear: "We're gonna have so much fun!"

"Mukbang, you take the boy." Colonel Granderson pointed a long finger at Julian.

Mukbang grinned and nodded, looking across the table at Julian.

"Playground and Cuckoo, take the girl." He pointed at Mamie. "Share nicely, okay?"

"Oh, we will," Playground said, his hands playing with the collar of his trench coat.

Cuckoo nodded, his eyes looking slyly at Mamie.

Whatever these two psychos had planned for his daughter, Jim had to stop it. He had to get out of this *somehow*!

"Plastic Monster, that leaves the matriarch to you. Oh," he pointed under the table, "go ahead and take Spawn with you." Holding his hands out, he addressed everyone. "I hope all of you are having a wonderfully devious Halloween. I'll see each of you downstairs when playtime is over." He turned to leave the dining room as his family rose from their seats.

"Let me talk to Jack!" Jim said, pushing his chair back with his feet, then turning it and rolling it forward. The wheels on the legs squeaked and proved to be not the easiest to roll. "Take me to Jack, Colonel, please!"

Colonel Granderson turned back, smiled at Jim, then said to the room, "Remember, do not kill them under any circumstances. It's not your place. Their hearts' last beat is for Jack and Jack alone." With that, he turned back to the entryway and was gone.

"Wait!" Jim yelled. "Take me to Jack now!"

"Calm the fuck down," Lady Spermjacker said, getting behind Jim and grabbing hold of the chair. "You'll get your moment with Jack, but right now you're mine." She giggled then and pushed him toward the entryway.

"Wait!" he yelled again, trying to whip his head around to speak directly to Lady Spermjacker but was restricted by the chains. "Please, take me to him now."

"Oh silly," Lady Spermjacker, giggling again, "you're so eager. But you'll have to wait!"

Jim looked frantically about the room, seeing Mukbang in his diaper, grabbing hold of Julian's chair; seeing Playground, the pedophile, and Cuckoo, the lunatic (as if they weren't all crazy), taking Mamie; seeing Plastic Monster in his orange suit, his fat fake lips stretching into a plastic smile as he grasped Mona's chair with one hand, his arm cradling the thing known as Spawn.

"Your world is about to change," he heard Plastic Monster whisper to Mona as he pushed her toward the doorway.

"Don't you hurt my family!" Jim yelled, straining against the chains helplessly. "None you bastards better hurt my family!"

"Or what?" Cuckoo said, grinning devilishly.

Mukbang chuckled, ruffling Julian's hair as he pushed his chair from the dining room.

Plastic Monster and Playground joined in with their own chortles.

"I'll kill you! I'll kill all of you!"

"Oh, Dr. Gibson," Lady Spermjacker said, squeezing his shoulders as she pushed him forward, "you won't be able to kill anyone when I'm through with you."

TWENTY-ONE

From the dining room, hearing the cries and pleas of his family all the way, Jim was wheeled to the right, through the kitchen, then past the house's foyer, then down a hallway where Lady Spermjacker hung a right into a small bedroom. Here, as everywhere else in the house, the room's light glowed orange.

The bedroom had no furniture aside from a single mattress at its center, free of sheets and stained with several reddish-brown blemishes. The floor around it was nothing but the floorboards seen throughout the house, old and creaky and in need of a good polish. The walls, contrary to the floor, were not bare.

The walls were covered in nails not fully hammered in, and hanging from the nails were all manner of sexual devices and implements of torture. There were things as innocent as vibrators hanging by looped strings; but then there were butcher knives and hammers, a circular saw and even a handheld, battery-powered mini chainsaw, the type used for small branches and little else. There was one draped window across from the entrance, then another door—presumably a closet door—on the wall to the right. But aside from those two areas, the walls were littered with Lady Spermjacker's playthings.

"We are in for a *fancy* time!" Lady Spermjacker said excitedly as she pushed Jim's chair to the mattress until the toes of his shoes bumped against it. "First, I got to get you out of that chair, doll."

At first Jim thought there was surely no way she'd said what he thought she said. That would be wishful thinking for sure. No way would this lingerie-clad woman—certainly no taller than five-five, and probably weighing a buck-twenty at most—was really going to unchain Jim, who was six-foot even and nearly two bills. He was a little beaten and bruised, sure, and a little queasy from dinner still…but he could take this woman one-on-one, especially with his life and the lives of his family depending on it. So surely she wasn't really planning on releasing him from the chains.

Yet, after releasing her grasp on the chair and closing the bedroom door, Jim saw Lady Spermjacker walk past him to a spot on the wall, where she plucked a small key from a nail. And here she was walking back toward him, neglecting to also grab a knife or a club or something to defend herself with.

"Now," she said, leaning in close to him, her breath smelling of the dead and devoured old woman, "you've got to be a good boy when I unchain you. No funny business! As much as you may want to slap me around like your little bitch, you best not do it. *You*, Doctor, are the bitch. Not the other way around. Got it?"

"What are you going to do?" Jim said, not wanting

to agree too quickly, which could cause her brain's deception alarms to ring.

She cocked her head at him, standing up straight again, and for a terrifying moment Jim thought she was turning back to the wall, perhaps to snatch the hatchet he saw reflecting orange light. But she just smiled and said, "We'll find out together!" Then she swept around him, gliding her hand seductively across the chains, still slick with vomit, then to his right shoulder and neck, where she squeezed gently.

She fiddled with the chains at Jim's rear. He heard the unmistakable sounds of a key sliding into a lock and the lock clicking open. Then the heavy sound of the lock hitting the floor. The chains loosened instantly but didn't fall away. And to Jim's utter shock Lady Spermjacker was now unraveling the chain from him. She was indeed releasing him from the only thing that had kept him from tearing her head off already. The chain could be used by her as a weapon, certainly, but not the easiest of weapons to wield.

Jim's mind was made up—when she'd removed the last of the chain from his torso, he would count to three in his head, seeding the belief in her that he meant to follow her orders, and then he'd pounce. He'd beat her first with his fists, then with whatever torture device on the wall was closest. And with her disposed of, he'd tear the house apart in search of the rest of his family. He could already hear wails and pleas from Mona. He had to move quickly.

The last of the chain slipped away with Lady Spermjacker still behind him, and Jim heard the chains shift as if she were getting the mass of metal straight in her arms.

One

He heard her take a step away from him, back toward

the door, the chains shifting again.

Two

Another step away, then the sound of a chain link dragging across the floor.

Three

Jim stood bolt upright, trying at the same time to spin around, to leap at the bitch, to tackle her and use the chain to strangle her to death. But his feet were locked in place, and when he spun, only his upper body and pelvis turned, his feet staying right where they were, and the sudden disparity between where his body wanted to go and his inability to bring his feet along caused him to fall backward toward the chair, his arms flailing. His tailbone hit painfully on the edge of the chair, sending it rolling away as he crashed to the floor.

He heard Lady Spermjacker moving again, moving toward him. But he didn't have time to look at her. He had to figure out what had trapped his feet and how to get out of it. The next few seconds could mean life or death. If he didn't get his feet unstuck, his whole family would likely perish tonight.

Quickly sitting up and trying unsuccessfully to bring his legs up, Jim looked to his feet and saw what was holding him in place. He felt them there now that he could them. But had he been asked just a few moments ago, he would have sworn there was nothing there, nothing holding him around his ankles. Certainly not some kind of green vine.

Sprouting up from between the floorboards at the base of the dirty mattress were green stalks, each sprouting a handful of large, lobed leaves, and each one wrapped around one of Jim's ankles, almost delicately. It instantly conjured images of the trumpet vine the Gibsons had growing in their own backyard, the way the thin stems

125

seemed almost magically to find pieces of chain link or small branches to encircle, carrying on its vining ways onward and upward.

Only, these two vines or whatever they were had not happened upon Jim's ankles by some magic of nature. Nor were they thin and pliable like the stems of trumpet vines, which could be easily snipped or redirected as needed. Grimacing, Jim jerked his legs backward then kicked them forward, twisting his ankles each time, and each time the mysterious vines didn't budge.

And now, Lady Spermjacker was standing over him from behind, holding that ball of chain.

"You dummy," she said, smiling down on him, "I told you not to try anything."

With that, she dropped the chain on Jim's head, ushering him from a sitting position to a sprawled-out lying on his back position, breathing through links of chain, grunting, his headache back worse than ever.

*

He'd passed out briefly after the chain was dropped on his head, and Jim vaguely pondered what kind of permanent brain damage he may have after the day of multiple knocks to the head. Always assuming he lived past this Halloween day, which seemed increasingly unlikely.

When he awoke he was on his back on the mattress, and the green vines that had ensnared his ankles had now multiplied. Leafy vines still held his lower legs, spread toward the corners of the mattress, and his arms were secured in the same fashion, extended like the arms of Christ on the cross.

Looking to his left, he saw the vine there slowly

encircling his wrist, almost gently so, and he felt the soft prickles of the vine's furs, leaves blooming larger as it grew. What the fuck was this? Some sort of plant with clear intent was securing him in place. Jim had read journal articles that suggested plants were much more intelligent than people realized—but this?

As he watched, more vines were sprouting from between more boards. The bedroom itself was quickly becoming a botanical garden. And the botanist of this particular garden—or at least the chieftain of this particular room on this particular evening at The Dark Side of Hell—was Lady Spermjacker, who stood at the end of the mattress where Jim's feet were, snipping a long, sharp pair of scissors in the air.

"Welcome back, Doc," she said, continuing to snip the scissors repeatedly. "For a second there I thought you were out cold, and that wouldn't be good. We kinda need you awake to get the full effect."

"Please," Jim said, feeling what was either blood or sweat dripping down his temple, "just—"

"Let you go?" Lady Spermjacker interrupted, grinning and shaking her head. "Come on, Doc. You need to get past that. It ain't happening." She snipped the scissors twice more, knelling down at Jim's feet.

"No!" Jim yelled, looking down that way but having his vision partially obstructed by the leaves of growing vines. What the fuck was going on? No more vines had made their way onto Jim or the mattress, but the floor...

"Relax," Lady Spermjacker said, "I'm just gonna get these burdensome clothes out the way."

The blades were sharp, slicing through his pant legs all the way to the waistband, where she cut through it and Jim's leather belt both. He tried to knee the woman once, but the vines seemed to anticipate this thought, holding his legs tight to the mattress. She removed his shoes and socks, tossing them aside, then cut through his boxers and the Tom Ford shirt Mona had given one Christmas before everything went to shit financially and maritally speaking. Lady Spermjacker laid open all the cut cloth, exposing Jim's body completely, the way any good ER nurse would do to a patient after a motor vehicle accident, though at least the nurse would cover his dick. Lady Spermjacker offered no such courtesy.

Tossing the scissors nonchalantly to the floor, seemingly oblivious to the vines, she stood at the foot of the mattress looking down on Jim with a frown, her fists on her hips. She pooched out her bottom lip.

"Don't I look good, Doc?" she said. "Don't you find me sexy?" She waggled her hips then grabbed and squeezed her breasts.

"Can't we just talk abo—" he started, but was quickly cut off.

"Why's your pecker all shriveled up like I don't excite you, huh? Ain't I a sexy slut?"

"What?" Jim mumbled. The answer to her question was fucking simple enough. There was no damn way he could get hard in the current situation. His life was in danger. His family's lives were in danger. Sure, this chick was scantily clad with about as perfect a body as any woman could ask for, but Jim Gibson wasn't exactly in the mood, no matter what his typical proclivities might suggest.

"You better get that dick hard, Dr. Gibson," Lady Spermjacker said, and then she started dancing seductively around the mattress, swinging her hips and letting her hands explore her body. The Halloween sounds that Colonel Granderson had put on earlier still played quietly, but Lady Spermjacker's moves seemed in in sync with a tune only she was hearing. She moaned to herself, then slipped a hand into the left cup of her bra, pulling her tit out and pinching her nipple. "Get hard, Doctor," she said, almost panting between words, dancing with her eyes closed, somehow navigating around the still-growing vines blindly.

Then she stopped, looking down on Jim and his limp dick with a scowl.

"I'm sorry," Jim said, actually forcing a weak smile. "It's just, you know..." He let his words trail off. Even in this absurd situation, there was a hint of embarrassment tugging at him.

"Well, I never!" She stomped her foot like a toddler and flared her nostrils at Jim. "Are you a fag, Doc? If I had a big ol' dick swinging around would that get you excited, huh?"

"No," Jim stammered. "Nervous, you know? I want to get out of here."

"Welp, you ain't going anywhere," Lady Spermjacker said, moving toward the wall. "And I don't have any of those get-hard pills on hand. But I do have an answer to our problem here." She took something off the wall, then twirled on the floor saying, "Wheeeee," then came to a stop, holding the device up for Jim to see.

It was a penis pump. Jim had seen them before, even bought one at a novelty store when he was in college, just to see what it would do, hoping like most guys that it would add a few inches of length and girth. All it did was provide an uncomfortable amount of pressure in his cock. This one, unlike the one he bought in his youth, did not have the hand pump. Rather, there was an On-Off button, meaning it was probably battery-powered, or rechargeable for all he knew. All he knew was he didn't want it coming near him. No amount of suction was going to arouse him on this day. He needed to get the fuck out of here and that was that.

If his face conveyed this message, Lady Spermjacker took no notice. She walked seductively to the side of the mattress and knelt down next to Jim. With her free hand, she reached over and thumped his dick, as if that would bring it to life. All it did was anger the pain that was already there from the turtle. She looked at Jim, pooching out her lip again.

"I'll fix it," she said, the frown quickly turning to a devilish smile.

"Please don't," he said.

But the tube with its rubber base was already being pressed to the flesh around his dead dick. Worried, Jim looked down at it, again embarrassed. Never in his life had his slong ever looked so pathetic. He felt ridiculous.

"Please don't," he repeated.

But now Lady Spermjacker, holding the tube tight against him, pressed the On button. Instantly, there was pressure and suction and growth. The circle of flesh in which his dick was at the center pooched upward, and the head of his cock pointed toward the end, the shaft growing veiny. It was uncomfortable from the start and getting worse, his cock going from as flaccid and lifeless as it had ever been to erect in a matter of seconds. His dick was stretching upward toward the electric pump, turning dark red. And suction power was increasing.

"Oh, I forgot to mention," Lady Spermjacker said, biting her lip, "I had Cuckoo fiddle around with the pump so it has more power. This sucker can turn a little shrimp winnie into a porn star's moneymaker."

"Please, turn it off!" Jim yelled, the pressure becoming beyond intense, as if his dick may explode at any moment.

It was going from dark red to purple and stretching near the end of the tube, which had to be nine inches long (Jim was typically a shade under six inches on his best days). Veins bulged, bluish-purple tributaries so unnaturally fat with blood that Jim could start IV in them with big, sixteen-gauge needles. It kept growing, stretching, becoming immensely painful.

"Oooo, you're getting nice and big there, Doc," Lady Spermjacker said, her hand still casually holding the penis pump in place "just like I like 'em!"

"Turn it off! Fucking turn it off!"

His arms pulled with every ounce of strength against the vines, but they held firm. He bucked his pelvis, trying feverishly to undo the seal or knock the pump out of the bitch's hand. He pulled uselessly with his legs, the vines there also staying true. And he screamed. He screamed with fear and agony he'd never felt, his eyes bulging at the penis pump and the monstrosity it was turning his dick into.

Then there was a burst of red within the tube, and Jim's screams grew more intense.

Only then did Lady Spermjacker release the suction.

"Awe, shucks," she said, hitting the Off button. She was smiling as she lifted the penis pump from Jim's body.

His cock slid out, purple and covered in blood, and flopped to his abdomen, visibly deformed, crooked, arching to the left like a badly broken arm. As Jim leaned his head over in horror, he saw that the right side of his member was split open like an overcooked hotdog wiener. Several veins along his dick appeared to have burst beneath the skin, causing bulbous hematomas along his shaft. Those could probably heal over time...but the open wound was a different story. The flesh of his cock had literally exploded open from pressure. Blood obscured his vision of the wound, but it was quite likely destroyed enough on the inside to never function properly again. Not without surgery, anyway.

*

"What have you done?" Jim muttered, tears—the first he'd shed on this day—dropping from both eyes.

"I was getting' all excited watching it grow, too," Lady Spermjacker said, tossing the penis pump amongst the vines and squatting down to get a better look at his destroyed cock. "It's still a lot bigger than it was, though, Doc. A healthy seven or eight inches, I'd say. Well maybe not *healthy*."

"You bitch! You crazy fuckin' bitch!" Jim slammed his head back on the mattress and wailed at the ceiling. His groin throbbed.

"I was gonna let you have your way with me, too. I was ready for a good pounding." She leaned towards him and thumped the end of his dick a second time, sending a shudder of pain coursing through his cock. "It's floppy now. Couldn't ride the bloody thing if I wanted to. What a shame."

Jim simply rested his head on the mattress and cried. His family was undergoing unknown tortures, his dick had been exploded, and death was almost certainly next. There was no escape from these vines of torment.

"I've got an idea, though," Lady Spermjacker said excitedly.

Jim opened his eyes, blinking away tears. When this chick got ideas, it was never a good thing. She was waltzing once more over to the wall, swinging those hips that would have driven Jim crazy with lust at one point in time. She took a hunting knife off the wall, one with a six-inch fixed blade, part of which appeared crusted with red stains. It could have been the knife Mother used to kill Sherry, Jim realized. Very likely was, in fact.

"Please, no more," Jim pleaded.

"Oh shut up," Lady Spermjacker said, licking the edge of the blade, perhaps tasting the blood there. Then, slipping her thumbs inside the band of her black lace panties, she slid them off her hips and let them drop to the floor, exposing a thin strip of brown pubic hair above a flawless vulva. "This could have been yours, Doc," she said, pointing at her pussy with the tip of the knife.

"For fucks sake, get it over with! Just kill me, you psycho! Get it over with!"

"Kill you?" Lady Spermjacker said, moving between Jim's legs and kneeling once more on the mattress. "That's not for me to do, Doc. I'll leave that to Jack. There's no rules saying I can't take your tallywhacker first, though!"

"What?!" Jim screamed. He began to protest, to assure her he would do anything if she would just stop, to the point he would empty his bank account and sign his house over to her if she would just put the knife down; but before he could get any of that out, it was too late.

With the fingers of her left hand, Lady Spermjacker lifted Jim's cock up by the head, stretching it painfully away from his body, and with the right hand she brought the knife smoothly across, slicing his cock off at the base. The movement appeared almost effortless, like a gentle wave of the hand; Jim's mind, amid all the horror, had time to think, *That's a sharp fucking knife.* And then nightmare flooded over nightmare as his dick was lifted away, leaving a bloody round patch and a ballsack at his groin.

"There we go!" Lady Spermjacker said, stuffing the

knife blade into the mattress and turning the severed cock over in her hands, blood streaming from it down her forearms. She was elated, her smile as broad and gleeful as possible.

Jim screamed at her, incoherent and wordless screams.

"Now watch this," she said.

And Jim did watch, his screams only faltering to take a breath.

Lady Spermjacker, still between Jim's legs, maneuvered into a sitting position, opening her stocking-covered legs up and laying them over Jim's still-restrained legs. With one hand, she spread her pussy lips, and Jim could see the glistening wetness within, even in this dull orange light. She rubbed gently at herself, moaning as she opened herself up. Then her other hand, bloody and cradling Jim's severed cock, moved toward her lusting snatch.

With a quickness Jim could hardly believe possible, Lady Spermjacker's hand delved into her pussy—thumb, fingers, cock, and all, past the knuckles and to the wrist. She gasped then squealed, her legs convulsing briefly atop Jim's. When she pulled her hand from her snatch, slick with her juices, it was dick free. She sighed and looked to Jim, biting her lip.

"It's my dick now," she said, then looked happily down at herself. "All mine."

For a moment she just sat, perhaps content with herself or perhaps pondering her next deed. All the while Jim wailed, though his complaints were going hoarse and decreasing in volume.

"Oh," she said after several minutes.

It came as no surprise to Jim when she snatched the knife back out of the mattress. And though screams heightened again for several moments when she took hold of his balls, squeezing them tight in her grip, it was almost a relief when she sliced his sack off, just a smooth, the pain burning through his lower abdomen.

"I got your nuts now, Doc," she said, thrusting the knife once more into the mattress and standing up. "Looky here!"

Crying, whimpering, Jim did look.

Standing there in her lace lingerie, with the exception of her discarded panties, Lady Spermjacker held Jim's testicles between her legs, as if it were her ballsack. Then, reaching a few probing fingers into her pussy with her other hand, she brought the tip of Jim's dick out of her dripping hole, sliding it out a few inches, so it hung there like it used to when attached to his own body.

"I got a cock and balls, Doc. Whaddaya think about that?"

Before Jim could scream and cry a reply, a loud sound issued through the house, almost like a moan or a yawn, but loud enough to shake the window panes and floorboards. The groan, or whatever it was, lasted no more than three seconds, yet the sound hung in the air even after it ceased.

The playfulness on Lady Spermjacker's face fell away, and she dropped Jim's testicles to the floor with a splat. His cock still hung there, swaying back and forth as she made her across the room, stepping over vines until she reached the closet door. She opened it, revealing blackness beyond.

"Time to go, Dr. Gibson," she said, leaning on the open door. "Jack beckons."

The vines tightened around his wrists and ankles, as others encircled his torso and thighs. He was being pulled now, toward the open closet. He screamed because there was nothing else he could do. In the last seconds before he was pulled into the darkness, Jim saw young pumpkins growing on the vines.

TWENTY-TWO

"This is my room," Mukbang said in that deep voice, smiling stupidly, his chubby cheeks seeming to push in on his smile like two dinner rolls.

Of it being Mukbang's room, Julian had no doubt— it bore all the hallmarks of a room a man such as Mukbang would inhabit—but it wasn't really a *room* at all; it was the kitchen pantry. It was a large pantry by most standards, and especially large for a house of this size, though it was without question bigger on the inside than the outside of The Dark Side of Hell suggested. The pantry was perhaps the size of a small bedroom, lit by a single orange bulb in the ceiling, with wood shelves along three walls and the door in the fourth. The shelves were far from bare, covered in canned goods and condiments of every sort, and in the far corner of the pantry were maybe a dozen open and empty cans littered on the floor with flies buzzing about. If Julian had to guess, this was likely only a day's worth of Mukbang's trash. In the other corner was what appeared to be a rolled-up adult diaper, also with flies circling. Right near this end of the pantry was a thin pallet of blankets with a pillow at one end—Mukbang's bed.

None of this concerned Julian, however. What worried him was that, after releasing him in a rather friendly manner from the chains around the chair, Mukbang had led him into the pantry and had him sit cross-legged in front of a propane griddle in the center of the floor. Now, Mukbang was seating himself on the other side of the griddle, across from Julian, grunting as he squatted down, at last bringing his diaper-covered ass to the floor with a loud thud. Mukbang held a pair of tongs in one hand...and a meat cleaver in the other. Worst of all, Julian's escape, the pantry door, was behind this mammoth of a man, closed.

Why the hell did I just walk in here? he thought, swallowing nervously. Though if he hadn't gone willingly, he certainly would have been forced into the pantry. And though Julian was certain he could outrun this tub of lard, he had a sneaky suspicion that getting out of The Dark Side of Hell was not a simple endeavor. It wasn't as if he could fight anyone with both of his hands blown to bits. They throbbed at the mere thought of them. His hands were still wrapped in dirty cloth, perhaps t-shirts, each of them with stains of red from bleeding. The pain ebbed and flowed in intensity, never coming close to going away completely. But one thing was for sure: he couldn't fight with his hands. His only way out of this mess would be with a clear lane to run in.

"Are you hungry?" Mukbang said, clutching the tongs and cleaver like two weapons of war.

"Um, not really," Julian said, trying to sound

pleasant and conversational. "I didn't throw up like the rest of my family."

"I saw that," Mukbang said, chuckling, causing the rolls of flesh of his torso to jiggle. "You like it here."

It sounded more like a statement than a question but Julian felt compelled to answer: "Um, it's alright. It's different."

As these words left his mouth, he realized how true they were. Julian was scared, without question. He was afraid for his life and afraid of whatever pain he'd yet to endure. He was even mildly worried about the safety of his family, though less so than he would have imagined. But this was the first day in years that hadn't been a mundane repeat of the previous day. Every day was always the same—wake up, eat, drink, shit, go to school, listen to teachers drone on about whatever, tap away mindlessly on a phone, eat, drink, piss, listen to more dumb teachers, go home, play video games, eat, drink, piss, shower, and go to bed. Even during the summer or on Christmas vacation, there was no shiny day of excitement, a day that held memories worth remembering. Those days without school consisted of more time on the couch and in bed and playing video games; little else. Prior to this day of debauchery, the most exhilarating event in the last six months was the *first* trip to The Dark Side of Hell, which wasn't exactly the pique of human entertainment.

Mukbang, setting aside the tongs, reached down to the griddle, which was maybe eighteen inches long and nine wide on its surface, and turned on the burner. Julian heard the instant hiss of gas, and seconds later he could feel the heat permeating.

"Why did y'all bring me and my family here?" Julian asked, wanting to keep Mukbang distracted from whatever he was planning.

"Jack told us to," he said, waving his hand a couple of inches above the griddle to feel the heat.

"Who is Jack?"

"Um," Mukbang said, looking toward the ceiling, scratching his chin, "he's God, I guess."

"God?" Julian said, tossing this around in his head. He didn't much believe in the concept himself, but he didn't figure Mukbang was speaking of a literal god. Rather, there was probably some kook around here calling himself Jack and proclaiming himself to be God or the second coming of Christ or whatever. He started a little cult on the outskirts of Mangle County, and now his disciples had kidnapped the family at his instruction.

With intentions of doing what? Julian wondered. Aside from making them eat the flesh of a diseased old lady, of course. Sacrifice? Burning at the stake of the unholy? God only knew. Or, more accurately, Jack only knew.

Mukbang nodded, confirming Julian's question of God. Then he reached to one of the bottom shelves, plucking a bottle of olive oil from the mix. He opened it and delicately poured a line of it across the griddle, where it instantly sizzled, the aroma filling the small room, almost enough to dispel the scent of shit and body odor. Then, replacing the oil on the shelf, he took down a shaker of black pepper and shook a healthy helping onto the griddle as well. Julian sneezed within seconds and felt his nose running.

Taking up the cleaver again, Mukbang inspected it, looking at his reflection in the metal, then flicking his thumbnail across the edge, making an almost inaudible *ting* noise. He smiled and chuckled a moment, then breathed in the air and looked at Julian.

"What do you want to eat first?" he said.

"I'm not hungry," Julian said. "We just ate." He shrugged and forced another smile.

"Okay," Mukbang said. "I'll eat first then."

He looked about the room as if seriously contemplating the decision. Julian glanced around too, feeling more nervous by the second. Why was he in here with this cannibalistic blob? Why was he, Julian, basically assigned to this guy? All things being equal, he would have preferred getting stuck with Lady Spermjacker.

Then Mukbang was staring at him, his cheeks spreading into a nefarious smile.

"What?" Julian said.

Mukbang set down the cleaver next to the tongs again, then reached his left hand toward Julian's right.

"What?" Julian said again.

"Give me your hand," he said.

Julian flinched and tucked both hands in his lap without thinking about it. "W-why?"

"I'm going to unwrap it," Mukbang said, as if this was the most logical thing.

"But why? It will hurt."

Mukbang chuckled again, a deep hearty laugh. "It don't hurt, boy. It don't hurt if you don't let it."

This made no sense to Julian. Of course it would fucking hurt, and there was nothing he could do about stopping that. He didn't *let* pain happen. Pain was the body's natural response to trauma, as Jim would have told him. Yet, for some odd reason, Julian wanted to listen. He wanted to believe Mukbang. After all, he was under the bastard's thumb at the moment. If he wanted Julian's hands unwrapped, those motherfuckers were coming unwrapped.

"Now, give me yo goddamn hand," Mukbang said.

Despite the change of words, his tone was still relatively calm. Julian guessed it would stay that way. This man had no reason to raise his voice. He held all the cards and he knew it.

Reluctantly, Julian ushered his right hand forward, about a foot over the griddle, feeling the warmth. Mukbang smiled and reached out, his fingers looking like thick sausages, and grasped Julian's wrist with one hand, and began unraveling the cloth with the other. It stuck briefly at times from dried blood, but came away easier than Julian figured, the last piece peeling away from his mangled hand with relative ease. It burned like hell, though.

Julian, who'd clinched his eyes shut when the unravelling started, breathed in and out deeply, trying to ignore the pain coursing through his hand and lower arm, then slowly opened his eyes.

It looked like something from a horror movie. His ring finger and pinky jutted out relatively unharmed, though looking paler than they should. His pointer and middle fingers were completely gone, with only clumps of red flesh and the white of finger bones showing just below the knuckles. Half of his thumb was still there, though no cop would be able to thumbprint him for any future run-ins with the law. A strand of skin maybe two inches long and barely wider than a toothpick hung from what remained of the digit, and it curled back on itself like Christmas ribbon.

Julian stared at it with weird fascination. It was like he was looking at someone else's wrecked appendage. He could feel the pain with the beat of his pulse and he could see that what was left of this hand was attached to his own arm, yet it somehow didn't feel real; it was almost dreamlike, looking at it. A thick drop of blood fell from where his middle finger once was and sizzled on the griddle.

He wondered if the day had gone as planned—if he'd succeeded in shooting up his school rather than watching masked gunmen do it—and he'd shot someone's hand apart, if they could be as calm and collected while looking at the damage as he currently was. If he'd shot Bradley Smith in the hand—or *hands,* for that matter—could he have looked upon them, realizing his football days were over, and not cried or screamed? Probably not. Julian felt a certain pride in holding back tears. He felt the same pride for not upchucking his dinner of Mother organs. He was stronger than his family and stronger than Bradley Smith too; maybe not physically, but certainly mentally and emotionally.

Mukbang was grinning at the revealed hand, his mouth hanging open, a single strand of drool swinging erratically around like a pendulum come loose from its fixed point. But he said nothing.

"Do you like it here?" Julian asked, genuinely curious, sniffling afterward, his nose still struggling with the pepper on the griddle.

"Of course," Mukbang said, seeming to come out of a trance.

"When did you come here? Have you always been here?"

Mukbang's smile suddenly fell away, his features becoming deadly serious. For a long stretch of a minute Julian thought he wasn't going to respond or even move, thinking something he'd said to this fatass had caused his inner workings to require reboot. But then he spoke, very slowly.

"Colonel Granderson brought me here, several years ago on Halloween. Me and my Mama and my two sisters." He paused, scowling—not at Julian but at something unseen—and then his face relaxed. "And now here I am," Mukbang said, as if his cheeriness had never left, "in The Dark Side of Hell, right the fuck where I want to be."

"What happened to your family, to your mom and sisters?"

"I don't talk about the before times," he said then smiled.

"Oh," Julian said, pondering. He set his uncovered hand gently in his lap. "Does someone get to stay every year? Like, do y'all do this every Halloween and one person gets to stay."

Mukbang considered this for a moment, scratching his chin. Then: "We do this every Halloween, yeah. We don't always keep no one. Most times, they all die."

The words hit Julian like a series of daggers to the heart. It wasn't as if he was mentally fooling himself, telling his brain everything would be fine; he figured the most likely outcome of this day was death. But to hear it from the horse's mouth made it taste a good deal different. *Knowing* rather than *thinking* he was going to die were worlds apart. But if sometimes they kept people...

"What makes you keep people?" Julian said, sniffling again. "Like, what's the, um, criteria?"

"Don't know," Mukbang said. "Jack decides that."

"Well, how do I talk to Jack? Maybe I want to join the family."

"I'll put in a good word," Mukbang said, then held his left hand out toward Julian's mangled right, as if to shake it.

"Thanks," Julian said, genuinely grateful, holding out what was left of his hand and allowing it to be taken.

With a quickness Julian didn't believe possible for

such an obese man, Mukbang snatched his forearm and slammed his hand onto the griddle, where it instantly sizzled. Before Julian could even issue his first scream, Mukbang's right hand swung around with equal swiftness holding the cleaver tight in its fist, hitting with expert precision just below the hand, chopping through the flesh and bones of the wrist, removing the hand completely with one brutal swing.

Then Julian did scream. It was the blood-curdling type of scream he'd only ever heard in movies, the type that would leave the screamer's throat raw and angry, stealing one's voice away for the next few days. He didn't even realize he was pulling, jerking away until Mukbang released his wrist, sending Julian sprawling to his back, where he pounded his head on the floorboards, his bulging eyes staring up into the blazing orange light.

His still-wrapped left hand prodded at the right stump, trying uselessly to clutch it or make his hand reappear or something else that would never happen. Blood spurted and streamed down Julian's arm into his shirt, darkening the fabric red from the sleeve to the shoulder to the back.

All the while, his hand sizzled in olive oil and black pepper.

Tears streamed down Julian's face. He sobbed and cried out and mumbled incoherence. He heard the sizzle lessen and heighten as Mukbang flipped his hand from one side to the other with the tongs. He smelled his flesh cooking, and were he not in immense agony, he might actually concede that it smelled quite fine.

Julian sniffled, sucking snot into his head.

"Sit up," Mukbang said, curtly now, free of the pleasantness he previously spoke with. "I said sit up, motherfucker."

"You...cut off my...*hand!*" Julian stammered, not budging from his back.

"Sit yo goddamn ass up before I cut something off you really fuckin' care about!"

Julian gasped and clenched his legs together. He wasn't exactly a sexual being but the thought of having his penis lopped off was about as horrible a thing he could think of. Would he even be able to pee if that happened?

Grunting painfully, Julian sat up, rubbing tears away on the arm that still bore a partial hand wrapped in rags. Through the crying fog, he saw his hand on the griddle; the part of his pinky and palm pointing skyward was browned from cooking.

"Blow them boogies on it," Mukbang said, pointing one of his sausage fingers at Julian's severed hand.

"What?" Julian said weakly.

"I said, blow those goddamn boogies on your hand."

He didn't question it any further. To do so would only anger the man further. Leaning forward, feeling the heat of the griddle on the underside of his neck, Julian positioned himself over the cooking hand and blew hard with both nostrils. He felt warm snot dribble across his upper lip but didn't feel or hear a drop. It would be a thousand times simpler to blow out a nice, fat, slimy booger if he had a free finger to hold one nostril closed. But he was fairly certain he only had two fingers left, and they were wrapped.

"None of it fell," Mukbang said, confirming what Julian figured.

"I know," Julian muttered, and he blew hard again, feeling the pressure of snot in there, both from the pepper and the allergies he always endured this time of year. He should be able to send a tea spoon-sized snot rocket flying to the griddle, but instead it rattled in his nose and clung to his lips.

Mukbang sighed loudly.

Julian sighed too, fresh tears coming to his eyes as he looked up.

He saw the gleam of the cleaver flashing in front of his face, reflecting orange light in mysterious hues. He felt the wind as it passed in front of his face and felt the hot rush of blood and pain, his eyes clenching shut, his face twisting into a grimace. And then warmth poured down the front of his face, and when Julian opened his eyes again, he saw his nose frying on the griddle the *outward* side up. A mixture of blood and snot dripped steadily over his hand and nose and across the griddle. It all hissed like a thousand snakes.

The more Julian screamed, the more he bled.

He barely noticed when the loud groan filled the house, shaking canned goods where they sat. He almost went willingly when the pantry door yawned open and the vines crept in, dragging him—squeezing him—past Mukbang, as he dined on Julian's flesh.

TWENTY-THREE

Spawn was riding in her lap as Plastic Monster pushed Mona Gibson through a door and into a room that looked like it belonged on a wholly other planet. That's what The Dark Side of Hell felt like—a different world entirely from the one where Mona Gibson was wife to Dr. Jim Gibson and mother to Mamie and Julian; where she cooked dinner three nights a week and got her nails done once every two and got her hair done as often as she could afford; where nights were often spent watching movies while doing laundry and drinking a glass of wine; where Mona made money with her body in a last-ditch effort to keep their house, and then found it was a profession she would need to continue until Jim could be the bread-winner again.

The bedroom was like that of a teenage girl on a popular sitcom. Unlike the rest of the house, the floors were carpeted here, plush and white, comfy to the soles of her feet as they grazed the floor from her chair. Bright pinks and purples caught the eye at every angle, from colorful lamps and dressers to the king bed with its velvety pink comforter. Posters decorated the walls, mostly of pop bands and artists, like Taylor Swift and Nsync and Boys 2 Men. There was even a poster of the cast of *Saved by the Bell*, with Mona's teenage heartthrob, Zack Morris, front and center.

Mona was unable to give any of this much thought, her brain doing little more than tucking this information away perhaps for further contemplation when the time was more appropriate. If she had thought deeply on it now, she might have perceived certain similarities between the room and the one of her childhood, her teenage years in particular, except for all the pink, of course. She might also have seen the similarity between what happened to her at sixteen and what was most assuredly *about* to happen to her now.

But Mona Lisa Gibson found it near impossible to withdraw her attention from the thing in her lap. Spawn was without question an abomination of nature. If God were real—Mona was on the fence about this—this thing wiggling atop her thighs, its tongue lolling out, dripping slobber across her flesh, lapping up the remnants of Mona's vomit that didn't make it to the dining room floor, was something only the most depraved demons in the deepest pits of Hell could conceive. It was both unholy and unnatural.

It simply should not exist, Mona thought.

As if to answer this thought, Spawn's wide, bulging eyes fixed on her face, and Mona thought she could briefly perceive a smile; though without cheeks, who the fuck knew? It made grunting, gagging noises at her, flopping its tongue—which looked five times longer than the tongue of any human baby—to the other side of its mouth.

Lying there, its flesh seemed to melt over Mona's own. There was too much of it around its torso, far too much for the frail frame it enwrapped, and the excess skin drooped all around it like those tubs of slime Julian had been mildly interested in for a year or two.

Its arms were contracted and elderly-looking, with the flesh here was more withered and tight. The shoulders moved frequently though, as if it wanted to reach for something but kept remembering that its arms were mostly useless. Judging by the calluses on its elbows though, Spawn used its arms and shoulders to crawl, if only to move it slowly forward, keeping that awful face off the floor.

The left leg looked fairly normal, almost like a regular toddler's leg. But the right leg—*Jesus Christ*—it looked like something one might expect to find in those cosmic horror flicks Jim sometimes watched, or like something you would stick on a hook and throw out to the depths of the ocean, in hopes of reeling in the one. Spawn's right leg appeared to be free of bones. It would lay limply there and then it would slither about across Mona's legs, like the backend of a snake or a tentacle, coming to a dull point at the end, rather than sprouting out to a foot. It was a fleshy, oddly orange tentacle.

But the thing sticking off its left abdomen, the large skin tag or whatever the fuck it was, was perhaps the worst, maybe even worse than its absent cheeks. *It can't be just a skin tag if it's twitching, can it?* Mona thought. Indeed, it was twitching, jerking about like a dying bug, with its three toothpick-sized appendages jutting out from it, then seizing too. Skin tags didn't have muscle, she was fairly certain. This thing did. It was as if another limb was trying to grow its way out of its belly. And with a thing like Spawn, was that so surprising?

Thank God it had a diaper on, secured tightly by the look of it.

"I'm going to unlock you now," Plastic Monster said from behind her, his voice high, feminine, Michael Jackson-like. Odd for such a large, imposing person.

Mona wasn't dumb. She knew what was in store for her when the chains came off. This bastard with his grotesquely smooth face, his plump fake lips, the escaped sea otter that appeared to sway back and forth underneath his orange slacks—he meant to rape her. There was no question about it.

But it wasn't happening. Not with her heart still beating anyway. She would claw this fucking prick's fake face off before she allowed his cock into her. She would fight him to the death.

The lock was undone, tossed onto a plush pillow in the room's corner.

Plastic Monster's arm passed over Mona's head as he unwound the chain, the fabric of his orange blazer brushing across her hair.

Mona vaguely realized she was still in nothing more than her own orange Halloween attire, her lace bra and panties. The lingerie was meant to make her several hundred bucks when this day started; now she would be fighting for her life with a thong up her ass and an uncomfortable bra cupping her breasts.

So be it, she thought.

The last of the chain was lifted away from her belly, where it left a pink imprint on her flesh. Before the chain left her field of vision, Mona snatched it and jumped up from her seat, propelling the disgusting Spawn thing to the floor, where it hit with a thud. Mona spun, holding onto the eighteen inches of chain she had under her control, seeing as she turned Plastic Monster looking back at her with mild humor, the pile of chains cradled in his arms like a bag of potatoes, his left hand clutching lightly at the piece Mona wielded.

He's letting me fight, she thought, realizing this was either a trap or a game. Either way, her decision was made—she was fucking fighting.

*

Mona swung the length of chain at his face, hitting the left side with a dull thud, a sound of impact with rubber rather than flesh. The strike split the smooth skin of Plastic Monster's cheek, but he didn't budge nor seem to be in pain. Indeed, his smile widened. And oddly, no blood emerged from the cut on his cheek—a bloodless open wound on the face, an area of the body packed with blood vessels.

Unless you've been under the plastic surgeon's knife a hundred times or so, Mona thought. She swung the chain back the other way, intending to hit the right side of his face this time. But as the length of chain came around, Plastic Monster dropped the bulk of it from his arms and caught Mona's onslaught in his massive palm. He eyed the chain curiously, turning it over in his hand as if looking for blemishes from the attack.

"I don't mind a little sadistic fun," he said, looking to Mona with crystal blue eyes, which were likely also fake, "but not when it sullies my face. I paid good money to look this pretty."

"Well, buddy," Mona growled, "I hope you have enough cash put away to pay for complete facial reconstruction!"

Dropping her end of the chain, she leapt at him, her hands open and fingers wide, as if she bore claws rather than fake nails, and aimed for his face. But he was quick. Releasing the chain from his grasp, he backhanded Mona midair, before she had a chance to lay a finger on him. The impact was powerful enough to send her sprawling to the floor, almost right on top of Spawn.

"You'd do well to just get on the bed, Mrs. Gibson," Plastic Monster said as he began slowly unbuttoning his blazer. "It'd be a whole lot easier on you."

"That's not fuckin' happening," Mona said, crouched over the carpet, wiping blood from her nose. "If you're wanting this pussy, you'll have to kill me first. Then it's all yours, you freak motherfucker."

Plastic Monster chuckled, removing his blazer and tossing it nonchalantly on a purple reading chair. He loosened his tie, a darker shade of orange than his blazer and much darker than the lightly colored vest, and pulled it from beneath his collar and over his head, in the process upturning a single clump of his slicked back hair, making him look like a giant, twisted Dennis the Menace. Then he removed his vest, throwing both garments atop the blazer.

Meanwhile, Mona had waited, stretching her back as she got herself off the floor and into a standing position. She wasn't waiting for Plastic Monster to prepare himself for battle, as if that was necessary for them to be on equal footing—they would never fucking be on equal footing. Rather, she was waiting for him to start pulling the white button-up shirt off. It fit him tight, and him pulling it from his bulky shoulders would surely provide her with a second or two before his arms were free again. And in those seconds, she would go for his neck with her hands and teeth, whatever it took to dig through his flesh and pull his jugular vein from his body.

She looked down briefly, seeing the thing that was Spawn crawling toward her on its elbows and left leg, the right one slithering along to its own beat. Mona shuddered and nudged the damn thing away with her foot.

"You remember when I smashed Spawn's diaper into her face this morning?" Plastic Monster said, smiling down at Spawn with incomprehensible affection.

Mona looked at him, breathing deeply. She saw that he'd ceased removing any clothes. He stood statuesque in his white shirt and orange slacks, his blue eyes slowly lifting from Spawn and meeting her.

"It was right before I knocked you in the head with the crowbar. Do you remember?"

"Of course I fucking remember," Mona said between gritted teeth. "Most disgusting goddamn thing I'd ever experienced. Until you and your sick family had me over for dinner."

He chuckled again. "The food, no matter what it is, always tastes good when you embrace Jack. When you embrace the depravity. But you'll never understand that."

"What the fuck are you talking about?"

"The diaper, it's nearing time for little Spawn here to make woopie again. He's pretty regular. Now, if you'll lay your sweet ass on the bed and take those panties off and spread your legs without a fuss, I'll leave Spawn on the floor. If you fight me, Spawn is coming to bed with us."

"You sick fuck, go Hell!"

"Good," Plastic Monster said without hesitation. "I wasn't going to leave Spawn on the floor anyhow."

He shot forward, surprising Mona, and wrapped one giant hand around her neck, his fingers so long that the middle finger curled nearly far enough around to touch his thumb. Leaning in close to Mona, an inch or two from her face, close enough that the horrid scent of Mother's consumed guts filled her nostrils, threatening to turn her stomach again, Plastic Monster spoke.

"In The Dark Side of Hell, no one gets their way unless they're in the family. *Our* family. *Jack's* family. Whatever you don't want to happen, Mrs. Gibson, it's gonna happen tenfold."

*

She felt her feet leave the carpet and felt the pressure increase around her neck and under her chin. Then she was flying as Plastic Monster heaved her across the room with one arm, landing her squarely in the center of his silky smooth pink bed.

Mona scrambled to get up, intent on jumping from the bed and going at him with everything she had. But as she went to sit up, she felt something prickly encircling her neck, tightening as she tried to move. Her hands went there frantically, pulling at whatever noose had gotten her. Though she hadn't thought there was room for anyone, someone had obviously been waiting on the other side of the bed with a rope. Yet when her hands grasped whatever was around her neck, it felt more plantlike, with the rubbery feel of a healthy vine. On one side there was even something with the soft, papery feel of a leaf.

"Let fucking go!" Mona screamed, pulling violently at the snare.

"It won't let you go," Plastic Monster said, standing at the end of the bed. "And you can't break it. Besides, you're wasting your energy. Save that fight for me, Mrs. Gibson. I like a rough woman. Long as she doesn't hurt my pretty face."

"I'm gonna fuckin' kill you!" Mona continued pulling at whatever had her around the neck, while also thrashing her legs and rolling side to side, trying anything to loosen the grip. But nothing gave. If anything, the tension around her throat increased, causing her to gasp.

Chortling again in his exaggerated *he-he-he* manner, Plastic Monster unbuttoned his shirt and pulled it off, easier than Mona thought, revealing a chiseled physique, likely bought and paid for through a combination of steroids and surgical procedures. His body was overly tan, almost orange in the way professional bodybuilders sometimes look.

Then he was kicking off shoes and pulling off socks, then undoing his belt and laying it on the bed. Then he undid his orange slacks and pulled down the fly. With a gentle tug, they fell to the floor.

Mona's frantic struggles withered to a terrified crawl when she saw Plastic Monster nude at the foot of the bed. If he fucked her with that thing, she could very well die from internal trauma. His cock, still soft, hung down to his knees, with veins bulging from the sides and down the center, and the head—*Jesus fuck*, she thought at the sight of it—was the size of a normal man's fist.

Bending down, Plastic Monster lifted Spawn from the floor, sniffing its diaper, nodding, then tucking the thing into the crook of his right arm. He smiled down at Mona.

"No woopie yet," he said.

Mona only glared back at him, then tugged at the thing around her neck again. He was right about one thing—it wasn't letting go, whatever *it* was.

Plastic Monster stepped over to a pink dresser, his giant cock swaying, then opened the top drawer, pulling out something small and black. Turning his head to Mona once more, he pressed whatever was in his hand, a button of some sort. It beeped briefly.

For a split second, his cock quivered as if seizing. Then it started growing, lengthening, hardening, coming up from between Plastic Monster's legs. The tan shade it had shared with the rest of his body grew darker as blood rushed in. If his dick looked massive before, now, continuing to grow, it looked like something out of a science fiction movie. This man, or whatever the hell he was, had a monstrous, fleshy serpent sprouting from between his legs. As it rose level with the bed, Mona half expected the fucking pee hole to grin at her, or perhaps open wide to reveal razor-sharp teeth or an all-seeing eyeball. It held there, strait out toward her, as if pointing the way. As Plastic Monster turned to place the button back in its drawer, she got a side view of the cock and gasped. It was impossibly long, and as the man turned, it audibly thudded against the dresser.

If I don't get out of this, this motherfucker is going to literally rearrange my insides.

"I'm not opposed to a little foreplay first," Plastic Monster said, waltzing over to the bedside, swaying his hips the way a curvaceous woman would. Reaching the edge of the bed, his cock hovered over the mattress, almost touching Mona's flesh, still lying more or less at the center of the bed

She didn't hesitate with the chance before her. Turning toward Plastic Monster, she took his massive member in her hands, the two hands combined not circling it fully, and dug her nails into it, pressing so hard that the joints of her fingers ached. She dug and pinched and scratched and pulled at the skin. The cock pinkened further, whether from the trauma of her attack or increased arousal, Mona wasn't sure. Because…Plastic Monster was moaning, as if she were stroking him gently and licking around his helmet with a wet tongue.

"That's it, my darling," he said, tilting his head back.

Spawn, still stuck in the crook of his arm, stared at her with those bugging eyes. Its right leg slithered upon Plastic Monster's thick forearm, almost lovingly.

"You like that, you fuck?" Mona screamed. "How about this?"

Yanking hard on his cock, Mona brought Plastic Monster stumbling closer, bringing the head of his dick within reach of her mouth. Pulling against whatever restrained her throat, she bit into his softball-sized dickhead, clenching her jaw as tight as her muscles would allow, screaming through her mashing teeth. She could taste the flesh and taste a trickle or two of blood; but it also tasted odd, rubbery, and somewhat vegetable-like.

"You're such a tease, Mrs. Gibson," Plastic Monster laughed.

Mona screamed, releasing the man's cock and proceeding to pound on his abdomen with fists coming in wildly from her supine position. Plastic Monster leaned onto the bed, bringing one knee onto the mattress, preparing, Mona thought, to mount her and have his way with her.

"No!" she screamed, bringing her lower half up, kicking both feet into the air repeatedly.

Plastic Monster avoided most of these blows with a smile on his face, enduring a couple of glancing hits to his pecks and arms. But one well-placed kick hammered Mona's heel into the underside of Plastic Monster's chin, causing his teeth to knock together loudly. He stumbled back, clearly dazed by the impact. Steadying himself, he grimaced, and Mona saw his tongue searching the interior of his mouth. Then, bending slightly at the waist, he spit out a single tooth amongst a glob of bloody slobber.

"You filthy bitch," Plastic Monster said, stepping forward, tossing Spawn carelessly to the foot of the bed and quickly seizing Mona's left ankle before she could kick him again. "What'd I tell you about my face?" Then, holding her leg straight up, he brought swift, powerful karate chop down onto Mona's knee.

Her knee instantly buckled inward, and as she screamed in agony, her hands reaching for her leg, Plastic Monster took the ankle in both hands and leaned into the break, folding her leg in the wrong direction.

Mona had felt pain before. She'd been hit by a car when she was fourteen, cracking two bones in her lower leg. She'd given birth to Mamie without anesthesia—not because she wanted to but because there simply wasn't time; she practically spit out her daughter the moment she'd moved from the wheelchair to the hospital bed. And she'd experienced two kidney stones in the last few years.

But this was an altogether different kind of agony. Mona read somewhere that knee injuries were the most painful. Now, she believed it. The piercing, cracking pain radiated throughout her entire left side.

"Fuuuuck!" she screamed, temporarily forgetting where she was and what was happening and what was at stake. All that existed was pain. Her face, still dirtied with dried shit from the morning capture, was red with anguish and tears spilled toward her ears.

Plastic Monster leaned over her, grinning, then delivered a hard backhand across her temple. Stars burst in her vision and a new ache pulsed in her head, blood trickling from a cut caused by the blow. Licking his fat, injected lips, Plastic Monster grasped Mona's bra at the sternum and jerked it quickly upward, breaking the clasps at the back and pulling the garment free. He tossed it to the floor. Mona whimpered as he moved lower and tore her panties off as well, revealing her smoothly-shaved nether regions.

"Is all that fight gone from you, doll?" he said.

"Fuck you," Mona cried, swinging at him wildly with a right hook. But he caught her forearm and, grunting, bent her hand back until the bones of her wrist snapped. As Mona screamed again, he tossed her arm back to the bed.

"I guess I better break your other arm and leg before we proceed any further. Spawn won't be able to have any fun if you're trying to fight him off."

*

Though consciousness never slipped away, it seemed to alter somehow, becoming different from the waking, understanding state of mind that normally dominated one's being, becoming, for Mona, a state of oblivion in which physical suffering and mental torment reigned.

Both of her knees were broken, making movement of her legs impossible without excruciating pain. Her elbows, too, were bent inward and deformed. Then Plastic Monster, in less than a minute, snapped each one of her fingers like they were twigs. Everything was quickly swelling and turning blue, with broken bones in some places pressing tight against flesh. None of the fractures, however, were open, as if by design, as if he knew this would be off limits.

He knows it could kill me, Mona thought in her haze of torture, *and he was told not to kill me.*

"Now for Spawn," Plastic Monster said, reaching for the thing still at the foot of the bed. As he reached, his cock brushed against Mona's left foot, sending a shiver of pain through that leg again.

She gasped and cried out. "Please, no more," she whimpered. All fight had vacated. Mercy was what she wanted. And if not mercy, then death. The gracious embrace of death felt unreachable, however, in Mona's current state of unmitigated torment.

"Oh don't worry, little Spawn won't hurt you any. Will you, Spawn?"

The thing made a wretched squealing sound, a sound of excitement.

"But let me assure you, Mrs. Gibson," Plastic Monster said, leaning down close to her, "if you hurt Spawn in any way, this will get oh so much worse for you. There are many more bones I can break without killing you."

"Gaaack! Ga-ga-gaaaack!" the Spawn thing screeched, a sputter of drool exiting its mouth and landing on Mona's breasts. It wiggled about in Plastic Monster's arms like any overly excited puppy.

"That's right, little one," Plastic Monster said, as if he had any clue what the goddamn thing was saying. "Here now, you want her to touch her nub? You want Mrs. Gibson to kiss your nub a little bit?"

Plastic Monster inched forward, his massive cock jabbing into Mona's side, and brought Spawn over her face. As he closed in on her, Mona turned her head, tears streaming from her eyes. The thing around her neck—she still had no clue what it was and had momentarily forgotten it was there—tightened as if by instruction.

"Turn your face toward us or I'll rip your flesh off," Plastic Monster said pleasantly.

Sobbing, Mona slowly did as she was told, and the thing around the neck loosened minutely. Turning Spawn over in his hands, Plastic Monster presented it to Mona like an offering, with its weird abdominal appendage pointing directly at her mouth. It quivered expectantly.

"Give Spawn's nob a little kiss," he said, his rubbery lips straining with a wide smile.

Releasing a gasp of horror, Mona kissed it, placing her full pink lips—lips that many men lusted over for many years—against the very end of the appendage, giving it a brief, delicate peck. Then she pulled her lips away, seeing the thing convulsing, the three thin limbs that jutted from it whipping around like boneless, flaccid snakes. Whether the spasm was intentional movement or some reflexive response, similar to an orgasm, Mona wasn't sure. All she was certain of was that she wanted Spawned removed from her sight immediately.

"Now put it in your mouth," Plastic Monster said.

"Please," she pleaded, and the endless tears rolled.

"Do it."

Spawn's cheekless mouth dribbled secretions across Mona's breasts. Its eyes bulged at her, seeming on the verge of popping out. A glob of snot fell from its nose and splatted on her neck. Its nob twitched as her mouth reluctantly opened. In the nob went, all three or four inches of it, until Mona's lips were pressed against the sagging skin of Spawn's abdomen. It quivered like a panicked rat in her mouth, the little tendrils slapping about over her gums and tongue. The appendage Plastic Monster called a nob felt mushy, like it was filled with wet sand. Mona wanted to retch.

"Now suck on that nub," Plastic Monster said.

Wincing, she sucked on the little protruding appendage, feeling it swell and jerk, one of the little tentacles tickling at the back of her throat. Spawn *gacked* repeatedly now, its drool spilling out across Mona's chest in bubbly strands.

Then she heard Plastic Monster moan and felt his cockhead slide beneath her ass cheek, prodding for her crack. This caused her leg to shift, sending pain splintering through her left side. Taking hold of her hip with the hand not holding onto Spawn, Plastic Monster pulled Mona's hip up, turning her lower half to the right, spreading her ass and exposing her asshole to him.

Mona screamed around the nub, both from pain and from what was undoubtedly about to happen to her. She could not fit this guy's dick in her ass. It was impossible. Her colon would rupture and she'd bleed to death from her butt. She pulled her mouth away from Spawn to scream frantically for him not to stick his dick in her ass, but she was stopped before a single word left her lips.

"Put the nub back your mouth! Suck on it till I say don't!"

After a muffled wail of protest, Mona's mouth closed once more around the quivering nub.

Plastic Monster's free hand came around Spawn's face, entering its mouth, gagging the thing, then scooping slimy drool into his palm. His hand then disappeared from view and Mona felt him coating her asshole and the end of his pecker with Spawn's drool. Then, grunting, he pressed forward, slowly at first.

There's no way it will fit, she thought.

It was like trying to shove a two-liter bottle into her ass. Never in her most graphically extreme cam girl videos had she attempted something so absurd. There were always weirdo watchers who wanted her to do crazy things—including a guy who repeatedly asked her to put a wine bottle in her pussy—but she wouldn't destroy her body for a little cash. Some cam girls who absolutely would if the price was right, but in some weird way Mona saw those girls as beneath her—they were the *whores* in the real sense of the word; she was just trying to keep from losing her house.

Now she was going to have her asshole turned inside out without making a dime, while sucking on a giant, moving skin tag.

Somehow, the end of his cockhead was pressing into Mona's rectum. She was opening up around it, the flesh there spreading painfully wide. She screamed around the nub then sucked in on it, screamed and sucked again.

Her asshole split on two sides. Not only did Mona *feel* the sudden tearing of skin, she *heard* it, like the ripping sound of denim. And just like that, his cockhead, the size of a softball or larger, was in her ass, and she suddenly had a pressure there that was only akin to giving birth. Under no other circumstances did this level of pressure exist outside of childbirth and being fucked in the ass by a giant dick manufactured in Hell.

Plastic Monster let out a wail of pleasure as he pushed in a few inches. Mona screamed too, unable to suck anymore from sheer agony. The nub wiggled and convulsed in her mouth, seeming to pulse with great intensity. It occurred to her—vaguely so—that perhaps it was climaxing.

It only took a few slow, extremely painful strokes for Plastic Monster to get his nut. His load exploded into Mona's ass like it was shot from a cannon. Perhaps more appropriately, a firehouse, because it shot into her with not only great force but also tremendous volume. She could feel the instant flood of pressure in her lower abdomen, and despite how tight her traumatized asshole squeezed on Plastic Monster's cock, cum still managed to spurt out around the rim, dribbling down her cheeks with the blood.

"Keep...sucking his...nub," Plastic Monster said between gasps of orgasmic bliss. His eyes cut to Mona's face, his jaw clenched, the veins in his neck and temple bulging.

Mona cradled the nub in her mouth, closing her crying eyes once more and sucked. The moment she did this, Plastic Monster shot one more load of jizz into her ass, groaning loudly. She felt as if her stomach might burst, as if this massive volume of cum would travel all the way up her esophagus and go blasting from her mouth and nose like a geyser. But somehow—perhaps it was the twist and turns of her intestines—the necessity to vomit a gallon of cum never presented itself.

At last, Plastic Monster pulled out of her, at the same time pulling Spawn away from her face. For a brief second, one of its little tendrils got stuck in her teeth but then it pulled free. Mona's asshole ached, and she could feel the mixture of blood and jizz oozing out of her onto the sheets. Yet the pain of her shattered knees and elbows still outweighed the rest. Mona didn't know how it was possible, but it was.

"Good girl, Mrs. Gibson," Plastic Monster said, his member slowly slinking down to the size of a small dog (apparently it didn't require the button to deflate). "Now, if you'll get Spawn off, we should be done here."

*

As it turned out, Spawn was a boy.

After destroying Mona's asshole and filling her guts with copious amounts of cum and making her suck on Spawn's weird deformity—all of which happened *after* each of her extremities were violently broken—Plastic Monster removed the thing's tightly-wrapped diaper, revealing a small, relatively normal-looking infant penis, which just happened to be steel rod hard.

Mona could only let out a brief sob. Fighting had long ago left her. It was an impossibility now. The prickly noose barely seemed to exist around her neck, as she had no desire to move. Every movement wailed with agony. She was broken in every way a person could be broken, from physically to mentally to spiritually. She was utterly shattered. She looked at Spawn hanging there in Plastic Monster's hands and barely saw him. Mona awaited death and nothing more.

Plastic Monster pulled on her left leg, rolling her to her back. She winced but didn't cry out, despite the pain. The moistness of the cum and blood-soaked comforter beneath her was expected. What wasn't immediately expected or understood was the feeling of a lump beneath her buttocks, as if she were lying atop a large meatball. Then it hit her: her rectum was prolapsed. This realization barely phased her. In her mind and then gone from it.

Moving to the foot of the bed, Plastic Monster pushed Mona's thighs apart. She groaned and scrunched her face, but said nothing. She breathed haltingly, like a child who'd cried for a long while.

"Here you go, little Spawn," Plastic Monster said, cooing at the thing. "This is what you want, isn't it?"

"Gack! Gack! Gaaack!" it said—*he* said.

"Yes, that's right, good pussy is what we all want."

He lowered Spawn between her legs, pushing his little pelvis against Mona's, guiding the tiny hard-on into her slit. Plastic Monster pulled Spawn back an inch or two, then pushed it back forward, thrusting for the creature, doing all the work for the damn thing. Mona barely noticed. All Spawn did was grunt and squeal and spill drool and snot all over her lower abdomen.

The creature started twitching, spasming in Plastic Monster's hands. Spawn's tentacle-like right leg slithered and slapped at Mona's inner thigh. The deformed appendage she'd been made to suck on wriggled crazily, as if struck with electric shock. Even his contracted, useless arms tried to tremble and flap about. And then Spawn was screaming. It was high-pitched, piercing even, sounding to Mona like the last dying screams of a murdered goat.

Then she felt it—the spurts of whatever substance this abomination of nature shot from its balls. It was brief but feeling it was feeling it.

Then Spawn vomited yellow bile across her stomach, and Mona smelled its sourness.

Then Spawn shot diarrhea from his ass, and Plastic Monster held him over Mona, showering her in it. The smell was as bad as before.

Mona just lay there, waiting to die.

"He always does that after orgasm," Plastic Monster said, a touch of affection in his voice.

When the loud groan shook the walls and green vines carried Mona into the darkness of a closet, she wished only for death.

TWENTY-FOUR

If only she'd dug the scalpel into her wrist this morning, opening up her flesh and arteries, spilling her life onto the tiles of her high school bathroom before any of this madness.

"Your mother ain't worth a damn sucking dick," Cuckoo said, leaning over her shoulder as he pushed her chair forward. "Hope you're better."

That was unlikely, of course. The only dick Mamie Gibson had ever sucked was Lance Bigsby's, and that was only for a few minutes because he was more interested in getting in her pussy. Mona, on the other hand, was a sex worker of some regard. She should be pretty damn good at the oral action.

The man known as Playground, in his tan trench coat, turned a corner in the hallway in front of them. It struct Mamie, not for the first time, that this house was much larger on the inside than it appeared on the out. It was no mansion by any means, but the hallways were long and there were a lot more rooms than anyone would think. When her family had made their way through it a week ago, they'd bypassed these halls, walking instead only through the larger corridors, which all connected in a jagged semi-circle back to the foyer.

Cuckoo turned the same corner and Mamie now saw ahead that Playground was pulling open a metal door, a door that reminded Mamie of a certain prominent horror film, one depicting the death of some young, weary travelers at the business end of a chainsaw. But rather than a red wall with some taxidermy decorating its surface, beyond the metal door was what appeared to be an iron scissor gate, and beyond that a small orange room, maybe six feet by six feet. It was, she realized, an old-fashioned elevator.

Sliding open the scissor gate, Playground waved his hand inward with a modest bow. Cuckoo, bowing in return, ushered Mamie's chair into the lift, then spun her about so she faced the elevator gate. There were only two buttons in this elevator, each with a brass nameplate above it. One read *Top Side*. The other: *Dark Side*.

Playground, entering the elevator after Cuckoo was situated behind Mamie, pressed the *Dark Side* button.

Mamie's heart was racing unreasonably fast. She was hyperventilating too. As a result, her fingers and toes felt fuzzy. In a normal situation—like if she was about to take a test she wasn't prepared for or had to give a speech in front of her class—she would recognize the panic attack for what it was and take the proper measures to slow down her breathing and get back on track. But in *this* situation, she hoped the panicked breathing would soon enough cause her to pass out. Not that a syncopal episode would help her in any conceivable way; quite the opposite, actually. But it would be an escape of sorts, if only briefly.

As the elevator purred and slowly moved downward, Cuckoo ran his fingers through Mamie's hair. It was tangled from the events of the day and had her vomit matted into portions on the right side, so Cuckoo's fingers snagged and pulled annoyingly at her scalp.

"You could be a pretty little thing, you know it?" Cuckoo said, his voice like gravel. "If you didn't have a little squirt growing in you. Colonel Granderson showed us the prego test you had in your pocket. You filthy thing, you."

Playground turned to eye her, smiling. "Oh, she's a pretty thing anyway. Young and petite. Looks younger than she actually is. Probably has little, perky tits under those chains." He tugged at his crotch through the trench coat.

Mamie swallowed hard, holding back tears.

The elevator stopped and Playground stepped forward, once more sliding away the scissor gate then pushing aside another metal door. Mamie briefly needed to squint at the brightness of the oncoming room, as Cuckoo quickly pushed her forward, past Playground, who also felt the need to roughly run his hand through her hair.

Her eyes quickly adjusting, she felt a sudden rush of dread. Mamie didn't know what she'd expected, if she expected anything, but it wasn't this. She'd been rolled into a room that belonged in a hospital. Or, more accurately, an old hospital, from fifty or sixty or more years ago. The walls were covered with light blue porcelain tiles, and there were white cupboards and drawers of several sizes. There was a stainless steel gurney along one wall, a gurney with a mattress along another, two circular bright lights hanging from the center of the ceiling, with long elbowed arms that clearly allowed the lights to be moved. And below the lights was another gurney, except this one was fashioned with stirrups.

At the opposite end of the room from where the elevator opened were two swinging double doors, with circular windows in each that would allow folks to peer through. Standing before these double doors was Colonel Gerald Granderson II with his top hat situated on his head, his arms clasped leisurely behind his back, and a smoking pipe in his mouth.

"Many pleasant greetings, Mamie," he said as Cuckoo brought her rolling alongside the gurney with the stirrups. "What do you think of my surgical room?" He looked about the room, bringing his arms out and gesturing to the walls.

Mamie didn't answer. The thought of being placed on that gurney terrified her more than anything. She'd had guns pointed at her and been hit in the head and been made to cannibalize any old lady's guts until she practically vomited her own guts into her lap. But none of that could compare to what would happen to her with her legs up in stirrups, with no one here to protect her. She wondered how far away her parents were. Would they hear her scream?

"I built it with my own two hands, wouldn't you know. Many, many years ago. Long before you were a shot of spunk mixing it up with an egg."

"Can I just go?" Mamie whimpered, and now the tears fell, her lip quivering like it hadn't in years, not since her dad spanked her for throwing a set of car keys at Julian when she was five and he was but two.

"I'm afraid that's just not possible," the colonel said, stepping forward, smiling down at her. "Jack asked for you. Just like Jack called upon me all those years ago. I was a surgeon in Chicago after leaving the army, would you believe it? A general surgeon to be exact, though I'd done a good deal of orthopedic surgery during the war. Met another surgeon there in Chicago. Became good friends with him. Man by the name of Dr. Sam Garfield. Ever heard of him?"

Mamie, barely listening because of her overwhelming terror, shook her head. She didn't know a Dr. Garfield and didn't give a shit about the colonel's stories of the good old days. She wanted to be left alone. She wanted to be gone from this horror house. More than anything, she wanted never to be placed in those stirrups. She would do damn near anything to stay out of them.

"Well," Colonel Granderson continued, "Sam was from this area, from Mangle County. When he heard I was driving down to Austin for a conference, he advised me to stop off in Twin Oaks on the way down, to go to a little place named Margie's Country Kitchen, and to try their pecan pie. And you know what I did, young Mamie?"

Mamie slowly shook her head.

"I did exactly as he suggested. I went to Margie's and I ordered a pecan pie. And let me tell you, that was a damn fine pecan pie. That, young Mamie, was October 31st of 1980. Halloween day. The day Margie's was robbed by three armed bandits wearing masks. I bet you can guess what the masks looked like, can't you?"

Mamie stared at him, the story slowly sinking in. Colonel Granderson was telling an origin story of sorts.

"Yes, Mamie, they were wearing pumpkin masks. And they weren't really robbers, were they? No, of course not. They were loyal subjects—or soldiers, you may say—the children—of the Almighty Jack. Just like me. They were there to take the feeder humans, like your dad and your mom and your brother. And they were there to take the conscript...like you, Mamie. Like Playground, like Cuckoo, like me."

*

"You see, Mamie, all of Jack's family," Colonel Granderson held arms out again, toward Playground and Cuckoo and the tiled walls of this room, apparently indicating everyone in The Dark Side of Hell, "are chosen. And so it happened for you. Congratulations."

The colonel paused, looking pleasantly down at her, sticking his pipe back between his cracked lips and taking a puff. Cuckoo patted her gently on her shoulder. Playground came around in front of her, beside Colonel Granderson, cocking his head curiously.

"What do you think, Playground," Colonel Granderson said, nudging Playground with his elbow, "do you think Ms. Mamie here is Dark Side material?"

Playground pondered for only a split second, then said, "Jack ever been wrong before?"

"Indeed not," the colonel said.

"Then I guess she's one of us."

"You hear that, Mamie?" he said, turning his attention back to her. "You're one of us."

Mamie again said nothing. She stared up at this man with a look of confused horror. Did he seriously think she would join *them*, this "family" of lunatics and murderers, who get their kicks eating diseased old women and shooting up schools and God only knew what else? Mamie might not be a picture of societal perfection but she certainly wasn't on level with these goons.

"There is a bit of an initiation process, of course," Colonel Granderson continued, "of which you've already been taking part. And, more importantly, *you* have been conscripted. You and only you. Not the, shall we say, *thing* growing inside you. That will have to go."

"What?!" Mamie suddenly gasped. If her heart was racing before, it damn near belted from her chest now. She looked frantically into the man's eyes for a sign of humor, but of course saw none. Nothing during the course of this day led her to believe anything was done in jest. He was as serious as stage IV cancer and just as deadly. "No." The word came out sharp and quiet. It was a demand but one she knew wouldn't be followed.

"Rules are rules, I'm afraid," Colonel Granderson said, taking a puff on his pipe then turning and moving back toward the double doors. "Don't you worry, though, Mamie," he continued without looking back, "I've fed Playground and Cuckoo and plethora of knowledge when it comes to medical procedures. They're getting pretty good at it. Successfully amputated a toddler's leg last month, as a matter of fact. Besides," and now he did turn around as he pushed one of the doors slightly open, "they're not allowed to kill you. Orders from Jack. So they'll be *extra* careful."

With that, Colonel Granderson was through the swinging door and out of sight. As the door rocked gently back and forth, Mamie saw darkness beyond, and a faint orange glow.

*

"Yeah, piggy," Cuckoo said, fiddling with the chain behind her back, "we won't hurt you too bad. Honest."

Playground chuckled, walking over to the double doors. He peered out one of the porthole-type windows then turned back toward Mamie, grinning widely, sticking his hands deep into the pockets of his trench coat.

The sound of a lock disengaging echoed off the tile walls. Cuckoo tossed the lock in the direction of one of the shelves with its many drawers, but the throw missed and the lock clanged loudly on the floor. The chain around Mamie immediately loosened. Not enough to shrug them off and make her way for an exit but enough that she could take a deep breath for the first time in hours. She wondered, if she were to get past these two psychopaths, would it be better to go through the double doors or back up the elevator?

"You wanna know what happened to me when I was initiated?" Playground asked, smiling wryly.

"Not really," Mamie managed to say, as Cuckoo looped the first length of chain from her body.

"Jack knows what you're into, right? He just knows somehow. So he knew—and the family knew—what I was into, that I like kids, right? So what do they do? Turns out, three of the feeder humans they'd taken that year—there were five of us total, me being the only conscript—but three of them were children. A two-year-old, a nine-year-old, and a twelve-year-old, all siblings."

He paused and looked over Mamie's shoulder, at Cuckoo, as another loop of chain was removed. She could pull out of the rest if she absolutely needed to but she wouldn't get very far.

"Cuckoo was there. So were Mukbang and Trespass—the fella your brother shot—and a lady named Dead Inside, who in fact died that day. They cut off an arm from each of those three kiddos before they went to see Jack. Then they brought those little kid arms to me.

And you know what they did? They fisted my ass with them. Then they slapped my face repeatedly with those dead, shit-covered hands." He chuckled again, shaking his head and appearing to wipe away a tear. "It was not the most pleasant thing, let me tell you." He looked up at Mamie and winked. "But here I am, alive and loving life. Living for Jack, just like you will."

Mamie looked at him with stunned silence. She couldn't let something like that or worse happen to her. The chain was almost completely off of her now; she would need to make a run for it and fight if she had to. Neither of these men were particularly large but large enough to take her down with one arm tied behind their backs.

"Cuckoo, why don't you tell her how you were initiated," Playground said.

Cuckoo groaned but cleared his throat and said, "Cut off my pinky toes and my pinkies." He dropped the length of chain he was holding and shoved a hand in front of Mamie's face. It was missing the pinky. "Made me eat 'em."

Playground laughed again, overly loud this time.

Cuckoo's hand disappeared from before Mamie's face and the rest of the chain disappeared.

"Hop on that stretcher there," Playground said, nodding toward the gurney with the stirrups. "Let's get that baby out of you. It'll make a nice dessert, I guess."

"Or we shove it up her ass and make her shit it out," Cuckoo said.

Playground shrugged, pooching out his lip. "Either works. Get on up there, girl." Then, looking down at himself, he undid the belt of his coat, followed by the buttons, the fabric parting several inches to where Mamie could make out the orange bikini thong beneath, and his pale white skin. He walked over to the corner near the metal gurney where there was a standing coat rack and slid it from his shoulders, revealing his bare ass cheeks.

Now was her chance. With Playground's back turned and Cuckoo walking over to a series of drawers, dragging a metal tray with him, Mamie sprang from the seat and, for no other reason than they were directly in front of her, she ran for the double doors, pumping her legs harder and faster than she could ever remember doing. She didn't have a clue what was beyond the doors but it had to be better than what was about to happen. There had to be a way out through there. After all, Colonel Granderson hadn't come down the elevator.

She was four steps away.

Three.

Two.

Something snatched her by the ponytail, which had somehow held relatively well throughout this entire ordeal. She was yanked back violently, losing her footing and crashing to the floor, the back of her head cracking hard on the tiles. Stars flashed before her eyes and she groaned. Scrambling to work herself into a sitting position, Mamie saw Cuckoo standing over her, her mind fuzzy from the impact.

"Piggy, don't run," Cuckoo said, and then she saw his pinkyless fist coming at her face.

*

How many times have I been knocked out today? Mamie wondered. But if she had brain damage, that was the least of her worries at the moment.

She'd been awoken with a splash of cold water to the face, and when she opened her eyes, standing to the side

177

of her was Cuckoo in his three-piece suit holding an empty pail that looked about two centuries old. He grinned crookedly at her.

"There you are," he said. "We didn't want you sleeping through the procedure."

"That's right," said Playground, coming into view wearing latex gloves, goggles, a facemask, and his orange thong, "you gotta be awake for the fun stuff or else it doesn't count. Jack's orders!"

Mamie groggily looked about herself, seeing that she still wore her black t-shirt but nothing else. They'd removed her jeans and panties and placed her on the gurney, restraining her legs in the stirrups with leather straps. Her wrists were also restrained with leather straps to the bedframe. She pulled gently at the straps, testing their tightness while trying not to alert her captors she was doing so. Both restraints seemed tightly secured to the bedframe but the strap around her right wrist felt slightly looser, as if she might be able to pull her hand free if she made her hand as small as possible and pulled with all her strength.

Playground stood between her legs and Cuckoo stood to her right, and beside him was the stainless steel tray. It was covered with medical instruments. Both bright surgical lights shown down on her private area, which hadn't been trimmed in a few weeks.

"Ready to get started?" Playground said.

"No, please!" Mamie pleaded, her voice cracking. "I'll do anything, just please don't do this."

"I wasn't talking to you, Mamie," Playground said, then cutting his eyes at Cuckoo. "You ready, Cuckoo?"

"Waiting on you, Playground," Cuckoo said, the corner of his mouth rising in a grin, his eyes on Mamie.

"What should her family name be after tonight? Abortion?"

"I like it. Or maybe *Un*bortion. Cause after we snatch this fetus from her woman parts, it's going back in her somewhere."

"*Yeah!* Unbortion, I like it!"

"Let me go!" Mamie screamed, pulling against all the restraints but finding no give, though her right wrist was definitely the most promising. Not that it would matter much if all she could do was swing around one free arm while the rest of her was restrained. Her captors would simply clock her in the head again and strap her arm back down, tighter than ever.

"We'll let you go, Unbortion," Cuckoo said, "when the time is right."

Playground brought a short stool on wheels between her thighs and sat himself atop it, stretching his fingers and arms as if he was preparing to exercise.

"Hmm," he said, leaning toward Mamie's privates, examining her while scratching at his chin with his latex-covered hand. "Very nice looking cunt we have here, Cuckoo. But I need to examine it a little closer. A little *deeper*, if you will."

Cuckoo chuckled.

"Let me go, goddammit! Let me go!" She jerked and kicked and pulled, her face growing red and sweaty.

"We have a combative patient on our hands," Playground said around laughs. "Good thing we have her secured tight. Now...speculum, please!"

Cuckoo's hand swept across the instrument table, scooping up the speculum, its shiny surface reflecting the lights as he handed it to Playground. The speculum always looked somewhat like a metal duck, to Mamie—a poking, prodding metal duck.

"Stop! Stop it!" she screamed, bucking her bottom before Playground had a chance to touch her.

"Make her stay still, Cuckoo, for fuck's sake!"

It took him barely a second to snatch a scalpel off the tray and swing it in Mamie's direction, bringing it less than an inch from her eye.

"You keep fighting, you lose your eyes," he said, bringing it even closer, to where when Mamie's eye blinked, her eyelashes brushed the polished steel. "You got that, piggy?"

"Yes," Mamie whispered, as if raising her voice to a normal tone would bring the scalpel into her head.

"Good," Cuckoo said, pulling back a bit, giving Playground a nod.

"Thank you, Cuckoo! Now let's get this party started!"

*

The metal was cold at first.

She flinched.

Tears trickled from her eyes.

The speculum spread her apart, slowly.

She pulled at the right hand restraint.

Hoping they weren't watching.

Spreading wider, painfully.

Too wide.

She was certain it would tear her flesh.

She sniffled and cried.

She was embarrassed.

As silly as that was, she was embarrassed.

Almost as much as she was scared.

"Curette!"

She sobbed at the word.

Pulled at the restraint.
It was in her, cold and rough.
Prodding.
Penetrating.
Scraping.
Hard steel on soft flesh.
"Jesus fuck, blood already!"
"Get me some gauze!"
The steel slipped away.
But not the pain.
She felt the blood beneath her.
Between her ass cheeks.
Her privates screamed in pain.
Her right hand pulled.
Pulled.
"Forceps!"
She sobbed again, louder.
She whispered a prayer.
Almost silent.
Her first prayer in six years.
Cold steel again, sharper, longer.
It poked and searched.
Jagged teeth opened and closed.
Tearing at flesh.
The pain.
It felt like fire.
Blood flowed.
She pulled at the strap.
He yanked, ripping, greedily.
Pain, intensifying.
Wet, squishing sounds.
Then the cold steel slipped away.
"Is that it?"
"I believe that's it, Cuckoo."

Then Mamie's hand came free of the restraint.

*

They hadn't been watching her hand or her struggle to free herself from the restraint. Though Mamie hadn't known at first what she would do with only one hand free, when it became clear she *could* indeed get it free, she quickly devised a simple plan, but that plan hinged on Cuckoo not moving any further away from her.

He leaned, just slightly, toward Mamie's pelvis when whatever Playground snatched from her snatch—presumably a never-to-be-born-alive fetus—having a look for himself, when her hand slid free. Cuckoo's hand, the one holding the scalpel stayed pretty close to where it had been, pointing at her face several inches away. And better still, now not only was his attention not on her hand, it was entirely on the bottom half of her body and the reddish, fleshy thing Playground was clutching in his forceps.

She didn't hesitate. Mamie's hand swung quickly across, catching the upper shaft of the scalpel and the bottom part of the blade, slicing open the webbing between her thumb and forefinger but also seizing the thing from Cuckoo's hand entirely. Before she considered the wound done to herself or how Cuckoo might react, she swung her hand again, back the other way, arcing it upward, toward the man's neck. He turned, a look of shock and anger upon his face, seeming to move in slow motion. Both hands were coming up, looking to grab Mamie's before it could do any damage. But she was faster. The blade of the scalpel, barely peeking out of her clenched fist, slashed across Cuckoo's neck, opening up skin and muscle tissue and his jugular vein.

Cuckoo gasped, stumbling back as blood poured across his suit. He pressed his hands there, trying fruitlessly to stop the bleeding. But the blood leaked between his fingers. The white shirt beneath his suit was entirely red in a matter of seconds. He looked to Playground with bulging eyes, looking for help that wouldn't—*couldn't*—come. Falling back against a series of drawers, he slid down to the floor, still clutching his bleeding neck, mumbling words Mamie couldn't understand.

Playground, when Mamie's eyes were on Cuckoo, had stood from the stool between her legs. Holding the forceps at his side, clutching a reddish clump of meat. He watched dumbly as his friend—his family member—bled to death, as if entranced by the scene.

Mamie, realizing she still had no way out of this without getting past or neutralizing Playground, and no way of getting past or neutralizing him with her left arm still restrained, looked frantically to that strap. It was a brown leather restraint, which buckled like a belt, and it was pulled extra tight. Fumbling with one hand to undo this would be difficult enough but doing it would also alert Playground to what the hell she was doing.

Instead, she corrected the scalpel's position in her right hand and brought it across to her left wrist, where she sawed into the thin belt-like strap of the restraint. It didn't cut near as easily or quickly as she was hoping, and she was sawing with such ferocity that she was repeatedly stabbing herself in the wrist, sending blood dripping to the floor.

"What the hell are you doing?" Playground said. "You're quite the fucking cunt, you know that?"

Mamie looked at him, still sawing, gritting her teeth, sweat dripping down her forehead. She pulled at the

183

restraint as she sawed, hoping to rip through the last bit of leather.

"You bitch," Playground said, slamming the forceps down on the instrument tray. There was a surgical handsaw there too, and he picked it up, waving it at her. "You're gonna regret that one. Let's see how you like walking around on one foot."

The strap snapped.

Screaming, Mamie's upper body shot up into a sitting position, both arms swinging toward Playground, her right hand still clutching the scalpel. Still standing between her legs, he brought his arms up defensively, and Mamie sliced across both forearms with the blade, flaying the flesh open.

"Arrrrgh!" Playground yelled, pulling his arms away from Maime as she brought her left fist hard against his cheek, causing his goggles to fly from his face. "You bitch!"

He brought the saw up, swinging it at her, slinging blood from his arms as he did so. Mamie fell back to avoid the hit but it grazed her chest, cutting through her t-shirt and the top of her breasts. Hitting the back of the gurney, she popped back up, ready for him.

As Playground swung back again with the saw, Mamie brought the scalpel in like a bullet for his face. She wasn't aiming anywhere in particular but it drove into and through the man's left eyeball, bursting it into a mess of blood and jelly, then popping through the other side of the socket.

Playground fell forward, spasming on top of Mamie for a moment, then slid to the floor between her legs with the scalpel still jutting from his eye. The saw hit the floor with a loud clang. Mamie pulled the speculum from her vagina—seeing the blood and gleaming metal of the duck bill—and dropped it, where it too clanged against the tiles.

Suddenly, a loud, rumbling sound erupted from the other side of the double doors, and the instruments left on the tray rattled like nervous children.

TWENTY-FIVE

Scrambling to get the restraints off her ankles, Mamie was certain one of the two men would pop up off the floor with a weapon in hand and do her in before she could escape. But neither did. Cuckoo was now motionless against the wall, his shirt drenched crimson. And Playground lay on the floor beneath her, his head and neck angled awkwardly against the base of the gurney.

Grunting, she moved her legs from the stirrups and planted them on the floor on either side of Playground's shoulders. She was unsteady as blood rushed back to her lower extremities, causing a somewhat painful fuzziness down there. But that pain was minuscule compared to the pain between her legs. She'd been sore after having sex the first time, but this felt like she'd been fucked repeatedly with a baseball bat.

Stumbling forward, trying to keep her bare feet from slipping on the combined blood of herself and Playground and Cuckoo, she scanned the room, listening for movement elsewhere. That loud sound that had come from beyond the double doors, a sound that was similar to the roar of a lion in Mamie's opinion, had stopped. But it still hung in the air somehow, like a threatening fog.

Her crumpled panties and black jeans were underneath the gurney. Mamie *knew* time was of the essence—that loud sound had to be an alert or call to action of some sort—but she'd be damned if she was going to run her way out of here with her bare ass showing. Bending down, her pelvic region screaming with every movement, she snatched her jeans from the floor and carefully pulled them on. She saw her Doc Martens and socks on the other side of the gurney but felt she didn't have time to waste with putting those on. Plus, her bare feet would be quieter on the wood floorboards in the house.

She'd made her mind up she was going back through the house. There was no way of telling what made the sound on the other side of the double doors without looking through one of the portholes, but it couldn't be fucking good. So she would go back up the elevator, try to avoid notice, and find her way out of the house. Then she'd go for help. She wanted to help her family, but if she tried to free them from their individual captors, it would likely mean a violent death for all of them. The best chance for any of them, Mamie figured, would be for her to find the closest help she could find. Perhaps she could sprint to the highway, if her aching groin allowed it, and flag down a motorist.

Taking a deep breath, Mamie shuffled around the end of the gurney, toward the elevator. As she did so, she bumped into the instrument tray and looked down. There sat the bloody forceps that had been shoved deep inside her. And in the locked teeth of the forceps, there was a lump of reddish meat that looked oddly like an amphibious creature of some sort. There were little arms and little legs and a head that was not quite round. It wasn't much longer than a silver dollar, but there it was: her offspring, as big as he or she would ever get.

Grasping the handles of the forceps, Mamie unlocked the teeth, freeing the thing. She picked up her dead fetus, turning it over in her hand, caressing it gently between her fingers, as if harm could be done. For a reason she could no more understand than the vast mysteries of the universe, she opened her front right pocket and dropped the fetus within, then patted the small lump in her jeans gently.

She was once more making her way for the elevator when the screams started.

*

It was the blood-curdling screams of her mom she heard first.

Her mom, Mona, who was prone to fits of rage when Jim or the kids pushed her too far; Mona, who didn't shed a single tear at her own father's funeral; Mona, who gave birth to Mamie without anesthesia—she was screaming and sobbing for mercy, from beyond the double doors of this surgical room from Hell.

Less than a foot from the elevator door, Mamie paused and turned to look at the double doors, trying to see beyond the porthole windows. But there was only darkness and that faint orange glow.

"Mom?" she whispered, though it wasn't a question of *if* it was Mona; it was a question of *what* was happening to her. What *had* happened to her already. Given what Mamie herself just went through, there was no fuckin' telling.

Then she heard her dad, Jim, muted at first then louder and louder still, until his wails drowned out Mona's. His screams of agony had words, like *NO!* and *WHY!* and *PLEASE!* Mamie had seen her father upset, in the times when substance abuse and gambling got the better of him and then some. She'd seen his spent tears drying on his cheeks and heard his weak promises of recovery. She'd heard his apologies, sincere and otherwise. But she'd never heard this.

"Dad." It escaped her mouth just barely.

Then more cries, younger cries, nasally and feeble. Cries of someone defeated and hopeless. Were those Julian's cries? Julian, who showed little to no emotion *ever*. Julian, who barely cried as an infant. It couldn't be Julian. But, then again, who else could it be but her brother, whipped into submission by this gang of tormentors?

"Jules," Mamie said, a name she hadn't used to refer to Julian in at least four years, not since before she was a teenager, when she decided for some reason it was too childish to call him such.

She had to go after them. Mamie couldn't let them die without fighting with her own life. Even a fucked-up family like hers deserved to be freed from the monsters within these walls. They deserved a fighting chance, anyway.

Mamie walked slowly across the surgical room, passing between the corpses of Playground and Cuckoo, and came to a stop before reaching the double doors. If she went through those doors—if she even looked through the windows—she needed to have a weapon or two. She was likely dead either way, but that fighting chance wouldn't be much if all she was swinging were her fists, still dripping with blood from her escape from the restraints.

Running to a set of drawers, Mamie began pulling them out, quickly and quietly inspecting their contents for usefulness. Most of what the drawers contained was different-sized and shaped forceps and scissors. There was also a series of implements that appeared to have the use of spreading flesh apart in different fashions. A variety of different scalpel styles were lined neatly in one drawer, but Mamie wanted something she could wield at a greater distance, if possible, and something that wouldn't need to be so precise. On the bottom row of drawers next to where Cuckoo sat dead, she found what she was looking for.

Wincing as she squatted down, pulling open the drawer, she almost gasped. Laying within was a stainless steel surgical hammer, around ten inches in length and heavy, she noticed picking it up. Beside where it had lain was a series of stainless chisels. Mamie grabbed the biggest one, which was several inches long and maybe an inch-and-a-half wide at the business end.

Mamie gripped the hammer in her right and the chisel in her left, knowing she needed to move quick, the sounds of her family's screams growing louder and more distressed by the second. There was another sound too: laughter. Colonel Granderson's family of psychopaths was laughing at whatever depravity was taking place. By the sound of it, all of them were out there beyond the doors—the fatass called Mukbang, the slut Lady

Spermjacker, the giant horror of cosmetic surgery Plastic Monster, and Colonel Gerald Granderson II himself.

Inching up to the double doors, Mamie peered out one of the porthole windows. She hadn't thought much about what she expected to see but if she had, it certainly would not have been what she presently looked upon.

Twenty feet on the other side of the double doors stood the colonel with his back turned, his top hat perched atop his head. He appeared to have his arms crossed as he watched what was going on in front of him. What was directly beyond him, Mamie couldn't tell, something orange and glowing. But to the right of him were his three still-breathing goons, facing the same direction, each looking about like they had at the dinner table, except for Plastic Monster, who was nude and muscular to the point of disgust, his ass looking like he could crush cans between its cheeks.

Beyond them, though, to the right and between the spaces of the colonel's family, was what perplexed and terrified Mamie. In what appeared to be a fairly large space, perhaps as large as a basketball court, there were green vines all along the floor—everywhere—and, more concerning, the vines were moving. They were slithering around somewhat in unison, like dancing snakes with large green leaves throughout growing from them. There were pumpkins too. Not many, but several sprouting from the moving vines. And there were bodies, writhing amongst the vines, screaming to get away.

It was her family. Mona's arms and legs were limp and twisted, her body jerking as she wailed. Jim was crying out, one arm fighting frantically against the plants. Julian, his weeping face poking out from amongst a cluster of wide leaves, his face forever mutilated. Noseless.

"Oh my god," Mamie said, her heart pounding, sweat still dripping from her head. None of this made a lick of sense. Moving plants carrying her severely injured family, while this collection of killer cannibals watched on, it was simply absurd, something out of a cheap horror flick. But it was happening, and Mamie knew what she had to do.

Silently, she pushed the door forward and stepped onto a dirt floor.

*

The dirt was cool, slightly damp, sending a chill from her bare feet through her body.

Mamie crept forward slowly, her eyes scanning the four individuals in front of her, her mind trying to ignore the screams of her family. For the first few feet outside the surgical room, there were no vines; but as she got closer, the reach of some of the vines came close to her steps, though they were thinner here. Yet they moved as if searching for something. Stepping over one slithering vine, Mamie's foot squished in the dirt, and when she looked down to see the reason for the new ground texture, she saw worms. Just below the surface of dirt now were earthworms by the hundreds, perhaps thousands.

Still, she inched forward. She would strike Colonel Granderson first. Though Plastic Monster was the strongest and Mukbang the heaviest, Granderson was their leader, unless this Jack person showed his face. So she would put the chisel to the back of his neck and bring the hammer down like she was looking to win the biggest prize at the fair. Maybe it would paralyze on impact and maybe it wouldn't, but it would sure as hell hurt. Then she would swing madly at the rest of them and make a run for her family, trying to get them untangled from the moving vines.

She was within seven feet now.

A vine brushed her ankle and moved on.

Five feet.

Worms squished beneath her feet.

Three feet.

She raised the chisel and hammer, preparing to take the shot in unison with her next step.

"Hello there, young Mamie," Colonel Granderson said without turning around, uncrossing his arms and reaching into his coat pocket, pulling out his pipe. "I take it Playground and Cuckoo won't be joining us for the remainder of the evening?"

Mamie froze, shocked that he heard her, even more shocked and dismayed that she no longer wielded the element of surprise. Peering to her right, she saw only Lady Spermjacker was looking at her. She cracked a smile over her shoulder then turned back to what was in front of her. And now, Mamie realized, she too could see in full what *was* in front of her.

Beyond Colonel Granderson and his band of misfits was a subterranean valley of sorts, a valley of crawling vines, all of which originated from one central location. The hub of that maze of vines burped out a laugh when Mamie's eyes fell upon it. It was a jack-o'-lantern, situated against the opposite wall of this underground room of soil and vegetation—a jack-o'-lantern the size of a dump truck, twelve to fifteen feet tall, its stem growing into the dirt ceiling with what appeared to be a mass network of roots that extended everywhere Mamie could see. The face of this massive Jack was cut in the classic Halloween style: two triangle eyes, one triangle nose, and a smiling mouth with several sharp teeth. Orange-yellow

193

light poured from its holes, not like there was a fire within, but some kind of mystical, glowing orb.

It was alive, Mamie realized instantly. It grunted and shifted in place and spit orange sludge from its carved mouth. The vines appeared to all grow from its base like a thousand vegetative tentacles. This was some kind of living organism; not simply alive like a plant but something that moved with intent.

"Say hello to Jack, Mamie," Colonel Granderson said. "The great and powerful Jack, the Jack who brought you and your family here. The Jack who picked *you* to be this year's conscript." He at last looked over his shoulder at her and smiled, his pipe jutting from his lips.

Mamie inched forward, the hammer and chisel at her sides. She'd lost the element of surprise but she still had to do something. Her family was suffering, each of them still being dragged along by the vines, closer and closer to Jack, its glow seeming to pulse at times like a heartbeat.

The colonel pulled a knife from his pocket and flicked it open, then bent down, his knees creaking, and cut a small pumpkin from the vine. He looked over at Mamie again as he stood. He cut a chunk of the pumpkin out and deposited it into his mouth.

"Want a bite?" he said to Mamie.

"Fuck you," Mamie said, gripping the instruments tighter. "Tell it to let my family go."

The colonel chuckled. "It's a bit late for that, I'm afraid. Jack made his choice long before you and your family arrived. Indeed, he'd picked the four of you even before your first trip here, a week ago. Didn't you find it odd that your father suddenly wanted to take everyone to a haunted house? It wasn't typical of Jim Gibson to want a night out with the family, now was it?" He paused but Mamie said nothing, only staring at him with contempt.

"Jack, you see, he calls to people. He can't exactly *make* people come but he has influence. And he has us, of course." He waved his hands at Mukbang, Lady Spermjacker, and Plastic Monster, who Mamie now realized was cradling that disgusting mutant Spawn in his arm. "We're here for Jack, to bring his feeder humans and conscripts. Jack wanted us to see you and your family before Halloween, so there'd be no mistakes come the big day. So he suggested, if you will, to your father that he bring y'all here for a haunted house experience." He chuckled. "The invitations were just a bit of a joke on my part." He laughed again and locked eyes with Mamie—his orange-tinted eyes. He held up the pumpkin again, an offering.

"Get that out of my face!" Mamie said, knocking the pumpkin to the ground with the surgical hammer. "I'm not any conscript. I'm not joining you and I'm not doing anything for that fucking thing. Let my family go!"

"You'll learn to love pumpkins," he said, turning a bit and pointing his pocket knife at her. "And I can't let them go, Mamie. From the moment he chose your family, the four of you were his. And since this morning, with y'all's capture, he's been *feeding* off of your family, including you. Oh, not feeding off fear like some silly Stephen King story. No. Jack feeds off depravity. Off wickedness. Off freakish lust and torture. Immorality of every sort. It's the deeds done *to* your family that feeds Jack."

"Let them go," Mamie said once more, her voice weak now. She needed to do something. Mona had stopped screaming now, appearing to have passed out or died. Jim's cries had turned to pathetic sobs. Julian's noseless face watched Mamie; he was the only one of them who realized she was in this subterranean room.

"On any other day of the year, Mamie, perhaps I could let them go. Depravity is typically enough to fill Jack's cravings. But Halloween is different, you see. On Halloween he requires flesh as well. He devours the feeder humans."

"What?!" Mamie said, looking wide-eyed at Colonel Granderson.

"That's how it g—"

Before another word could leave Colonel Granderson's mouth, the surgical hammer smashed into his cheekbone.

TWENTY-SIX

Colonel Granderson's head rocked back as he yelled out, his top hat flying off, the pipe falling from his mouth, the knife slipping from his grasp.

As the colonel fell, Mamie turned to her right, seeing Mukbang, the closest to her, coming at her with his arms raised high, either intent on wrapping them around her or slamming both heavy hands upon her head. With his giant abdomen left unprotected, Mamie stepped forward quickly, placing the chisel against his belly, and slamming the hammer into it. The seven-inch chisel was driven into Mukbang's fatty flesh like a nail into a two-by-four. Only a circle of stainless steel shown in his dark skin, just above his belly button. A single drop of blood hung from the wound as he stumbled backward to the dirt and vines, crying out, landing with a loud thud.

Lady Spermjacker just avoided being crushed by Mukbang's fall. As Mamie tried desperately to change direction and go after her family, Lady rushed her. Seeing the colonel's knife on the dirt, Mamie bent down and scooped it up, then spun toward Lady's oncoming assault and smashed the hammer into her knee. She too yelled out and fell to the ground. Mamie meant to drive the knife into her but Plastic Monster was coming her way.

"Back off!" Mamie screamed, holding both the pocket knife and the hammer up in the air.

But Plastic Monster came at her, jogging, his giant cock swinging about, still holding Spawn in the crook of his arm.

Mamie swung maddeningly at him with the hammer. His height was such that her aim was basically for his chin rather than his head, but when Plastic Monster leaned back to avoid the blow, the hammer instead struck Spawn at the very top of its head.

The thing's skull was brittle, and the surgical hammer smashed through it like plate glass. A burst of soggy brain tissue, blood, and what had to be puss exploded from the hole made by the hammer. Spawn whined for only a brief second, its whole body quivering, the tentacle leg whipping about like a fish out of water. And then it went limp.

"Spawn!" Plastic Monster screamed in his high-pitched voice, stopping his advance on Mamie, holding the little creature up close to his face.

Mamie didn't pause to fight any longer. Her family, beginning with Jim, were getting dangerously close to Jack's mouth. She had to get there with the pocket knife and cut them out of the vines and do what she could to get them out of there.

But she barely made it two steps before she herself was enwrapped in vines. In barely the blink of an eye she was covered in them. Vines held her legs motionless, held her arms out to her sides, unable to swing her weapons, and small vines even wrapped around her skull and pulled her eyelids back, so she could watch what was about to happen.

Her dad, Jim, was there now, at the monster's mouth, the mouth of the thing known as Jack. The vines were ushering his naked body toward its open, glowing gullet. Jack grunted three quick grunts—laughs, Mamie thought.

"No!" she screamed, tears falling.

As Jim sobbed, Mamie noticed the bloody absence of his penis and thought how horrible a situation he must have endured. The vines carried him like the corpse he was.

"Christ Almighty, Mamie," Colonel Granderson said, stepping alongside her, blood dripping from his face, "I think you broke my cheekbone."

"Hurt my fucking knee too," Lady Spermjacker said, limping up on the other side of her. "The newbies always gotta act tough."

"Same as you did, Lady, same as you," the colonel said. "Too bad for Mukbang, though. I was hoping to keep him a while longer."

Mamie could hear the fat bastard still weeping behind her, not dead but certainly dying from massive internal bleeding.

"Help my dad!" she screamed.

"There's no helping him," Plastic Monster said, coming up alongside Lady Spermjacker. "Just like there's no helping Spawn." He tossed the little thing to the dirt and vines before them, apparently done mourning.

The vines, they seemed to move in slow motion, yet Jim moved like a raft on the ocean, sliding across. Mamie didn't have a chance to protest further. Her father was dumped into Jack's mouth despite her screams.

His screams heightened for only a second or two as he passed beyond the pointed pumpkin teeth and into the glow. He screamed as his skin instantly melted away and then he gurgled as liquified flesh filled his throat and lungs. Muscle, fat, and organs bubbled and melted, becoming a pink froth, which also quickly disintegrated into the glow. Then only Jim's skeleton was left, and it too became thin and brittle before dissolving completely, as if it was never there at all. The whole matter lasted no more than ten seconds.

Mamie wailed, unable to look away from the horror.

Mona was next, the vines ushering her into Jack's maw, her broken limbs flopping around awkwardly. She made not a single protest. As she went in feet first, her eyes gazed sadly toward her. Mamie thought there was an apology in those eyes—*I'm sorry, Mamie; I'm sorry I failed you*. And then she was melting away, her flesh gone from her bones and her bones gone seconds later, hissing like a simmering soup on a hot stove.

Mamie tried desperately to look away, to close her eyes, to do anything but watch the destruction of her family. But the vines held.

Julian looked desperately from Mamie to Colonel Granderson to Lady Spermjacker and Plastic Monster, as if expecting one of them to lend him a hand. The red hole where his nose once was dripped blood down to his chin. He muttered something, directed, Mamie thought, either at her or the colonel, but it was drowned out by Jack groaning as its vines pulled Julian toward the glowing abyss. He too was dumped in, his clothes sizzling away like they'd never been there. Then, just like their parents, Mamie's brother melted into nothingness there in the heat of the giant jack-o'-lantern.

In less than a minute, her entire family was dead.

*

She was so stunned by seeing them killed that she barely noticed when the vines loosened around her arms and legs, and released her eyelids, allowing her to blink. They slipped away completely to the dirt floor, and there Mamie stood between Colonel Granderson and Lady Spermjacker, with Plastic Monster on the other side of her.

Mamie still held, she realized, the surgical hammer and the colonel's pocket knife. None of the others seemed concerned by this in the least, as if watching her family die would somehow take the fight out of her.

A loud, rumbling belch issued from Jack, so monstrous a sound that the ground above and below Mamie's feet quivered. Jack sagged slightly then, like a satiated man after a big Thanksgiving dinner.

"Halloween often demands a hefty toll on our family, just as it did yours, Mamie," Colonel Granderson said without looking away from the glowing jack-o'-lantern. "Tonight you lost your father, your mother, and your brother. We, Jack's family of The Dark Side of Hell, lost Playground and Cuckoo tonight, and Trespass and Necrosis earlier in the day. Not to mention Mother's offering at dinner and Spawn's passing. There is a lot of death yet a lot of joy for the sacrifices made for Jack. Rest assured, he is pleased and will reward each of us in kind over the next twelve months."

"All the pleasures you desire will be yours," Lady Spermjacker said, turning to look at Mamie.

"Every meal can taste like filet mignon, if you like," Plastic Monster said. "Like rotten corpses, for instance. And every orgasm will flood your being with unlimited ecstasy. Whatever animalistic cravings your body has, Jack can deliver. He has that power, Mamie."

"If, of course, you eat of his pumpkins," Colonel Granderson said, and now he did look at her. "You must first eat of his pumpkins, Mamie."

"We need to give this girl a new name," Lady Spermjacker said. "*Mamie* ain't gonna do. Sounds like an old lady name."

"Indeed," the colonel said, chuckling, "a new name is in order."

"Playground and Cuckoo already named me," Mamie said, her face stern as she watched the glowing flicker of Jack's face.

"Is that right?" Colonel Granderson said, sounding surprised. "What name did they suggest?"

Now all three of them were looking at Mamie. Playground and Cuckoo had decided on *Unbortion* for her name, after doing what they'd done, strapping her down and violating her, ripping a fetus from her loins. An unborn person who she only learned about for certain that morning, though she'd suspected it for a few weeks. How long ago that seemed, sitting in the bathroom stall with a scalpel to her wrist. A bit ironic, she thought, that she would end up taking others' lives with a scalpel later on. She wanted death that morning, and now here she was contemplating death again, though of a different sort.

"Suicide," Mamie said, never diverting her eyes from Jack.

"Suicide?" Colonel Granderson said with approval in his voice.

"That's right," Mamie said, "They called me Suicide."

Mamie sidestepped quickly toward the colonel, gritting her teeth and raising the pocket knife in the air. Before he had a chance to dodge or block the blow, she brought the knife down, burying it to the hilt in Colonel Granderson's neck. His screams were wet and gurgling as he fell.

Mamie did not hesitate. Spinning, she drove the stainless hammer into Lady Spermjacker's face as she came at her. The blow hit her directly in the mouth, shattering and dislodging several teeth. Lady fell to her hands and knees, spitting teeth fragments into the dirt.

Plastic Monster's big palm came soaring through the air, smashing against Mamie's head and ear, knocking her to the ground, her head ringing like a bell. But she moved swiftly. As Plastic Monster stepped closer to her, hovering over her, Mamie came to her knees, swinging the hammer in the same motion, swinging it with all the power she could muster, swinging with one target in mind, swinging it at Plastic Monster's fist-sized dickhead.

It was a perfect hit.

His cock swung backward between his legs with the blow, and his subsequent high-pitched scream was worthy of envy from horror movie scream queens the world over.

Mamie popped to her feet, not bothering to look at Lady Spermjacker or Colonel Granderson to see whether they were up and coming at her again. As Plastic Monster clutched his cock with both hands, Mamie raised the hammer to deliver a blow a bit higher, and she saw past the man, seeing a stone staircase in the dirt wall not far away.

Mamie swung and the hammer cracked against Plastic Monster's chin, coming loose in her hand and slipping away. She did not pursue it. As Plastic Monster cried out and stumbled backward, she bolted for the stone stairs. The vines slithered beneath her feet but did not grasp at her legs or in any way attempt to suspend her fleeing.

"Come back here, you stupid ungrateful bitch!" Lady Spermjacker screamed.

But Mamie's feet hit the cold stone of the steps and she flew up them two at a time, bursting through the wood door at the top. She was in the kitchen, she realized instantly, and without a thought she bolted past an open pantry where a griddle sat on the floor, still sizzling.

She found the foyer without difficulty and rushed through the door, out onto the porch, where her bare feet came sliding to a sudden stop. The brisk autumn breeze was cool against her sweaty flesh. The dry leaves of the trees rustled nervously. Mamie panted, her heart pounding, her eyes watching the swaying kerosene lantern hanging from a hook above the porch, the orange flame flickering. A slight smile arose on her face.

Grasping the kerosene lantern off the hook, Mamie looked back into the house. No one yet appeared in the entryway in pursuit, though Plastic Monster and Lady Spermjacker would likely both be along soon. Colonel Gerald Granderson II was hopefully dead. Mamie threw the lantern at the wooden floorboards just inside the house and it shattered, instantly spreading several feet of fire across the floor.

Mamie turned, taking a deep breath of cool air, and leapt from the porch into the night.

*

She was only halfway down the winding, dirt driveway when she stopped running.

Mamie wasn't sure why she'd stopped at first but then she felt the little lump in the pocket of her jeans, remembering what was in there. Reaching into her pocket, Mamie brought her offspring out just as a gust of wind whipped around her. It was wet and mushy in her grasp. Opening her hand, she looked curiously at the thing. With limited light, the flesh and blood of her offspring appeared black. She thought of throwing it amongst the leaves and running onward, but then the crackling sound of fire stole her attention.

Turning around, Mamie saw between the trees the rising fire of The Dark Side of Hell. The house was built of old, dry wood and it was burning well. She laughed silently. Then something else caught her attention.

To the left of the house and the trees that partially obstructed her vision, was the vast pumpkin patch. There amongst the pumpkin patch was a scarecrow, the firelight illuminating its attire of overalls and a flannel shirt, stuffed with straw, just like scarecrows seen everywhere. The scarecrow's head, though, was a jack-o'-lantern with triangle eyes and a triangle nose and a sharp-toothed smile, and it glowed from within. It glowed at Mamie.

She stared at it for a moment, then looked down at the fetus in her hand, then back at the scarecrow. She nodded slightly.

"Happy Halloween, Jack," she whispered, putting the fetus in her mouth and chewing.

The wind howled and the fire roared as she walked toward those glowing eyes.

A WORD FROM THE AUTHOR

If you read this fucked up little book then chances are pretty good you've read other tomes of the same genre. Chances are probably pretty good you're into indie horror. If that's the case, good for you! If you're new here, welcome to the club! We need all the loyal readers we can get. And if you're one of those loyal indie horror readers, you may have noticed the names of some of the characters in *The Dark Side of Hell* sounded somewhat familiar. You may have wondered if I purposely named certain characters after certain books. The answer is *YES*, I most certainly did. The book titles that earned character names in this novel are as follows: *Playground* by Aron Beauregard, *Cuckoo* by M. Ennenbach, *Spermjackers from Hell* by Christine Morgan, *Mukbang* by Alyanna Poe, *Plastic Monsters* by Daniel J. Volpe, *Trespass* by Chris Miller, *Necrosis* by Rayne Havok, *Dead Inside* by Chandler Morrison, and *Unbortion* by Rowland Bercy Jr. If you haven't read these books, get on that. I wouldn't have made their titles into characters if they weren't damn good!

ABOUT THE AUTHOR

Patrick C. Harrison III (PC3, if you prefer) is an author of horror, splatterpunk, and all forms of speculative fiction. His other works include the Amazon best-selling novelette *100% Match*, the Splatterpunk Award-nominated novella *Grandpappy*, the genre-blending novels *A Savage Breed* and *Vampire Nuns Behind Bars*, and many others. You can find his work on Amazon and his Etsy page, PC3Books. Follow his FREE substack, PC3 Horror, for updates on his fiction and other horror goodness.

20470119R00130